NARUTO'S STORY

STORY

Uzumaki Naruto

and the Spiral Destiny

Masashi Kishimoto
Jun Esaka

CHARACTERS

Uzumaki Naruto

Seventh Hokage. Hero of Konohagakure.

Uchiha Sasuke

Naruto's rival and friend. Formerly of Team Seven.

Uchiha Sakura

Sasuke's wife. Formerly of Team Seven.

Hatake Kakashi

Sixth Hokage. Master of Naruto's Team Seven.

CONTENTS

Mitsuki
Orochimaru's son. Konohagakure genin.

Uchiha Sarada
Daughter of Sasuke and Sakura. Konohagakure genin.

Uzumaki Boruto
Son of Naruto and Hinata. Konohagakure genin.

Nara Temari
Older sister of Fifth Kazekage Gaara. Shikamaru's wife.

Nara Shikadai
Shikamaru and Temari's son. Konohagakure genin.

Uzumaki Himawari
Boruto's younger sister. Inherited the Byakugan.

Kankuro
Older brother of Fifth Kazekage Gaara, Temari's younger brother.

Gaara
Fifth Kazekage of Sunagakure.

Kurotsuchi
Fourth Tsuchikage of the hidden village of Iwagakure.

Hozuki Suigetsu
Originally from Kirigakure. Works at Orochimaru's base.

Karin
Sensory Radar shinobi. Works at Orochimaru's base.

Orochimaru
Former Konoha shinobi. One of the Three Great Shinobi.

Kanhen Furieh
Administrative director at the Kengakuin international research institute.

Ameno Chihare
Scholar at the Kengakuin international research institute.

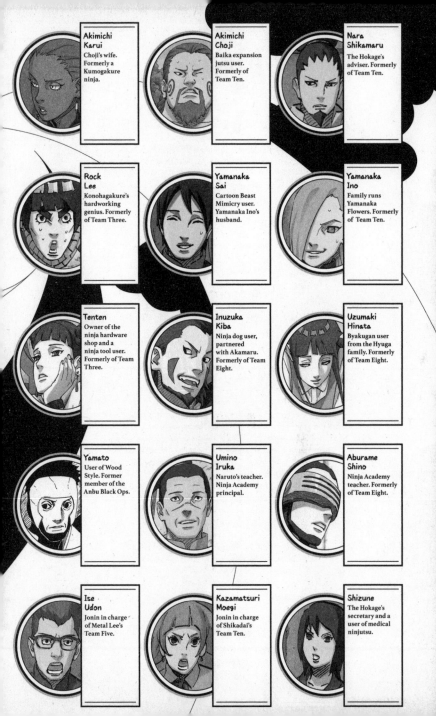

Akimichi Karui
Choji's wife. Formerly a Kumogakure ninja.

Akimichi Choji
Baika expansion jutsu user. Formerly of Team Ten.

Nara Shikamaru
The Hokage's adviser. Formerly of Team Ten.

Rock Lee
Konohagakure's hardworking genius. Formerly of Team Three.

Yamanaka Sai
Cartoon Beast Mimicry user. Yamanaka Ino's husband.

Yamanaka Ino
Family runs Yamanaka Flowers. Formerly of Team Ten.

Tenten
Owner of the ninja hardware shop and a ninja tool user. Formerly of Team Three.

Inuzuka Kiba
Ninja dog user, partnered with Akamaru. Formerly of Team Eight.

Uzumaki Hinata
Byakugan user from the Hyuga family. Formerly of Team Eight.

Yamato
User of Wood Style. Former member of the Anbu Black Ops.

Umino Iruka
Naruto's teacher. Ninja Academy principal.

Aburame Shino
Ninja Academy teacher. Formerly of Team Eight.

Ise Udon
Jonin in charge of Metal Lee's Team Five.

Kazamatsuri Moegi
Jonin in charge of Shikadai's Team Ten.

Shizune
The Hokage's secretary and a user of medical ninjutsu.

NARUTO NARUTO RETSUDEN © 2019 by Masashi Kishimoto, Jun Esaka
All rights reserved.
First published in Japan in 2019 by SHUEISHA Inc., Tokyo.
English translation rights arranged by SHUEISHA Inc.

COVER + INTERIOR DESIGN Shawn Carrico, Jimmy Presler
TRANSLATION Jocelyne Allen

Published by VIZ Media, LLC
P.O. Box 77010
San Francisco, CA 94107

Library of Congress Cataloging-in-Publication Data

Names: Esaka, Jun, author. | Kishimoto, Masashi, 1974- artist. | Allen,
Jocelyne, 1974- translator.
Title: Naruto's story : Uzumaki Naruto and the spiral destiny / Jun Esaka,
Masashi Kishimoto ; translation by Jocelyne Allen.
Other titles: Naruto retsuden. English | Uzumaki Naruto and the spiral
destiny
Description: San Francisco, CA : Viz Media, 2023. | Series: Naruto retsuden
| Summary: "When Naruto is no longer able to use chakra, the shinobi of
Konoha come together to help him. Even Orochimaru offers to assist with
scientific ninja tools. While directing the people around him with all
the dynamic ferocity of a mighty whirlpool, Naruto stands tall, facing
this trial with an unbreakable spirit!"-- Provided by publisher.
Identifiers: LCCN 2022039045 (print) | LCCN 2022039046 (ebook) | ISBN
9781974732593 (paperback) | ISBN 9781974738144 (ebook)
Subjects: CYAC: Ninja--Fiction. | LCGFT: Light novels.
Classification: LCC PZ7.1.E816 Nat 2023 (print) | LCC PZ7.1.E816 (ebook)
| DDC [Fic]--dc23
LC record available at https://lccn.loc.gov/2022039045
LC ebook record available at https://lccn.loc.gov/2022039046

Printed in the U.S.A.
First printing, March 2023

viz.com

SHONEN
JUMP

Prologue

"Mom, is the Lord Hokage going to come out soon, maybe?"

Her small hand clutched the hem of the skirt fluttering next to her face.

"I'm sure he will. We'll be able to see him soon," the mother said gently, turning her gaze toward the sacred site at the top of the hill.

Inside of the humble sandstone shrine, the Seventh Hokage himself was meeting with the daimyo of the Land of Kizahashi. A large crowd had gathered below to get a glimpse of the hero on his first visit since his appointment as Hokage.

The air along the smooth diagonal of the slope was rippling with excitement, and smoke arose from orange flames. However, no one was burning anything. This hill had been aflame for more than its four thousand years of recorded history. The inextinguishable fire was seen as both a blessing of the gods and the curse of a demon. And it had been the subject of worship and fear since ancient times.

When the Fourth Great Ninja War ended and a pact among the Five Great Nations brought peace to the world, news of the mysterious, eternally burning fire reached the Sixth Hokage, Kakashi, and a survey team was dispatched to investigate. Using both science and ninjutsu, a vast pocket of natural gas was discovered to be seeping out from beneath the hill, which was ignited by the surface heat, creating the eternal flame.

The eternal bonfire moved the air, creating a breeze that constantly rustled the dark grasses and the neat petals of the gently blooming violets.

The Seventh Hokage and the daimyo of the Land of Kizahashi emerged from the shrine exactly on time. The conference had ended without incident.

"Hokage!"

"Lord Seventh! Over here!"

"Do the Rasengan!"

Cheers rang out from the crowd gathered at the foot of the stairs.

In response, the Seventh Hokage raised his arms as if to actually produce the Rasengan, and the Konoha guard behind him hurriedly pushed them back down.

"Lord Hokage, please don't use the Rasengan like that! This is a matter of national defense!"

"Come on. It's fine. Just let me," the Seventh Hokage said sulkily, and then reluctantly lowered his arms.

Uzumaki Naruto.

He was top shinobi of Konohagakure, the young leader appointed to the position of guardian of the Land of Fire, the Seventh Hokage. His bright golden hair flashed like lightning, his clear blues eyes were reminiscent of ramune soda in summer. He was in his mid-thirties, but there was a boyish innocence in his unaffected manner.

It was established fact that he was the Jinchuriki of the Nine-Tailed Fox, but his face was less fox and more tanuki. Not only were his eyes, nose, and mouth large, but his face was very expressive—every part of it seemed to be in constant motion. It wasn't just his face either; his every move was exaggerated, drawing people's eyes to him. He was a charismatic leader with a personal magnetism that attracted everyone to him, and the way he was beloved transcended everything else.

Accompanied by several guards, the Seventh Hokage slowly began to descend the stairs built into the diagonal slope of the hill. The red carpet at his feet had been a special order especially for this day, and it extended the entire distance to the entrance of the airship parked near the base of the hill.

Naruto stopped abruptly halfway down the carpet, squinted his eyes as though the sun's glare was too strong, and looked off into the distance. He could no doubt see the far-off skyscrapers piercing the clouds. The faded field at the foot of the hill ended abruptly at the border of the capital city, where the sharp, inorganic elements of the urban landscape took shape.

The Land of Kizahashi had developed rapidly once it began exporting its gas to the Five Great Nations, which used it as fuel for their large transport vessels. The GDP had increased seventeen-fold over a decade, new infrastructure was created, and there almost seemed to be too many social services—the average life span of its citizens had increased by twenty years.

The land was swimming in money. What it lacked was legends and lore. Stories of heroes.

"Lord Hokage, how did you find your stay in the Land of Kizahashi?"

Reporters surrounded the Seventh Hokage, shoving microphones in his face, when he finished descending the stairs.

"I'm glad I got to experience the development of the Land of Kizahashi firsthand. I came before as a guard with the survey team that was dispatched by the previous Hokage. Just seeing the development of the Land of Kizahashi since then made the trip worth it."

Shrieks of "Please come again!" greeted the Hokage's comments.

"Ha ha! Well, find me another reason to!" the Hokage replied, laughing, and the crowd broke out into applause.

The people of the Land of Kizahashi adored the leaders of the storied ninja villages. They especially revered the leader of Konohagakure, the Hokage. At a time when smithing was the main industry and most people still lived hand-to-mouth, the financial assistance from Madoka Ikkyu, the Land of Fire's daimyo, and the Sixth Hokage, Hatake Kakashi, was a lifeline that lifted them out of a depressed economy and into a new industry of refining Kizahashi gas. Not long after, the economic growth of the Land of Kizahashi had surpassed that of the Land of Fire, and the grateful citizens had never forgotten the country that had once uplifted them in their years of poverty.

The more people loved the Seventh Hokage, the more influence he possessed, and ultimately the more enemies he inevitably had. No doubt the person who commissioned the assassination of Uzumaki Naruto was one of those enemies.

Staring intently at Naruto as he spoke with the media, Aze Yanaru narrowed his eyes. A rogue ninja and expert assassin, he had changed his appearance with the Art of Transformation and gotten quite close to the Hokage.

A basic principle of assassination is to kill when the target is alone, but Yanaru often chose to work among crowds. He liked a surprise attack surrounded by an indeterminate number of eyes, a feat made possible thanks to a four-person cell that took full advantage of the art of Multiple Shadow Doppelgangers.

His Kekkei Genkai allowed Yanaru not only to gain the accumulated memories of any doppelganger who disappeared, but also to share those same memories with the remaining avatars. During an assassination, the very nature of which was unpredictable, being able to secretly exchange information like this was a huge advantage.

His doppelgangers—A, B, and C—were already in place and locked onto the Hokage. Meanwhile, there were only three bodyguards around the Hokage.

The promised payoff was enormous. If he could pull off this job, he, his children, and even his children's children would spend the rest of their days in leisure.

Yanaru looked around at the crowd at the foot of the hill and exhaled his tension.

The Seventh Hokage's life meant money. Way more than that Kizahashi gas.

Yanaru's doppelganger A was hiding in the thick branches of a tree and looking down on the Seventh Hokage.

The luxurious goat hair carpet upon which the Hokage walked was extravagantly dyed with sappanwood. Not only was his pathway blatantly obvious, but the area surrounding him was completely wide open. The exposed fields with essentially no blind spots practically screamed, "Go ahead, kill me." The Hokage's right hand, Nara Shikamaru, had no doubt argued vehemently against such a route, but the Kizahashi side had pushed it through, saying something about how this hill was the most sacred place in their country.

Doppelganger A touched the rifle in his hand and reminded himself of how it worked.

The cutting-edge photon gun supplied by their employer was designed to attack from a distance with a forty-thousand-watt excimer laser beam. Because the heat of the laser was instantaneously transmitted from cell to cell, even if the beam only grazed the tip of a hair, the target's body temperature would shoot up uncontrollably within minutes, and the target would internally combust.

Doppelganger A readjusted his hands on the grip and lifted his face to find the media peppering the Seventh Hokage with questions.

"The Land of Fire also imports gas from the Land of Wind, yes? I know they've long had a strong relationship with the Land of Fire, but some people are saying that the two countries favor each other and are trying to lock Kizahashi gas out of the market. What do you think about that?"

"Whaaaat? Who's saying that? No way," the Hokage replied firmly. "The Kazekage's an old friend, but we set that aside for any country-level negotiations."

"Then you're saying there's no favoritism?" the reporter persisted.

"Nope, none. We import tons of gas, but that Gaara guy won't even give his pal a discount," Naruto riffed.

Laughter rose up from the media crowded around the visitor. The Seventh Hokage deftly evaded the pushy questions, whether through his own natural personality or careful calculation.

Doppelganger A glanced down at his watch. Ten minutes had been allotted for this press conference. The Hokage would soon start down the carpet that had been made specifically for him and move toward his airship, leaving himself wide open.

That's when A would make his move. He impatiently tightened his grip on the photon gun and licked his dry lips.

Hyooo! A slice of wind grazed his cheek.

"Hm?"

He looked to the side as the air squealed, and a dagger plunged into the trunk of the tree.

Stunned, A moved around to a position behind the trunk and crouched down.

He was here to take out the Hokage from a safe distance, but for some reason, he was the one now under attack.

When and how had he been found out? Who threw that dagger? Where were they?

His mind reeling, he shoved a hand into his jacket to counterattack.

The leaves above his head rustled and one dropped onto his knees. A gloved hand grabbed A's neck from behind while he gripped the photon gun.

"Huh?"

He lifted his face and met sleepy eyes, like those of a mountain goat. He saw the face of a lazy-looking man, half covered by a cloth. He'd more than seen this face before. This man was...

"Hatake Kaka—"

A kunai sank into A's throat before he could finish saying the name. The tip of the twisting blade severed bone and flesh, and droplets of blood spurted up and spattered the foliage.

Poof!

Wrapped in smoke, A disappeared without a trace.

As A disappeared, his memories flowed into the heads of the original Yanaru and his two remaining doppelgangers B and C.

The last sight A had seen was the worst possible thing imaginable.

Hatake Kakashi. With his lazy, drooping eyes and his perceived lack of drive, he seemed like a sloth of a man at first glance. But not a single shinobi in the Five Great Nations was deceived by this appearance. As the former Hokage, Hatake Kakashi was simply too well known.

For one thing, he had been the one to dispatch the Kizahashi gas survey team, so his popularity rivalled that of the Seventh Hokage in the Land of Kizahashi. With so much fame, how he could go unnoticed by a single person in a crowd was proof of how adept Kakashi was at erasing his aura.

Yanaru remembered reading a story in the newspaper about how Kakashi had been living a quiet life after retiring as the Sixth Hokage, spending his time onsen hopping. Yanaru never dreamed that the shinobi was still active in the field and working as a guard for the Seventh Hokage in addition to that.

B kicked slowly at the dirt with his straw sandals.

Hatake Kakashi had deliberately missed hitting A with the first kunai in order to allow Yanaru's doppelganger to see his face. He had most likely meant to intimidate Yanaru. His initial attack had been a warning for third-rate assassins to quietly abort the mission and walk away since they didn't stand a chance against *the* Hatake Kakashi.

What an annoying man, using his celebrity like that. Had he cut A's head off just for show, to demonstrate that he was more powerful than Yanaru and to scare them away?

B pulled his hands into his sleeves and wiped the sweat away.

Calm down. Don't let your nerves show on your face. He'll find you if you're acting unusual.

B inhaled and held the breath for a moment before parting his lips to let it out. But something blocked his mouth.

"—!!"

An arm quickly followed, wrapping around his neck, and he was yanked up, a whistling breath escaping his panicked lips.

B grabbed the wrist of whoever was covering his mouth.

Slender. A woman's wrist.

Trying to get away somehow, B kicked his left leg back, but his kick was ill-judged. The tips of his toes kicked up and hit nothing but empty air. And then, as if his assailant was taking advantage of this opening, she kicked the leg he was standing on out from under him. He flailed forward until she caught him with a leg, and B was pinned in place, unable to move.

Deprived of oxygen, his brain slowly shut down.

In his hazy mind, he could vaguely feel something soft touching his back. So it *was* a woman.

A female ninja guarding the Seventh Hokage alongside Hatake Kakashi. A woman with enough skill to finish him off with no one in the crowd any the wiser, an immense strength that brooked no resistance.

Haruno Sakura?

He was sure of it, but B never found out if his guess was correct. Without so much as a glimpse of the face of the person strangling him, B turned into smoke and disappeared.

What was going on? Wasn't the guard detail supposed to be light?

C panicked. Hatake Kakashi and Haruno Sakura—two extremely capable, extremely famous shinobi—were both guarding the Seventh Hokage. They could go ten against one in a direct fight with these two, and they still wouldn't stand a chance.

The Seventh Hokage was slowly walking toward the airship.

Calm down, C told himself. *I'm a doppelganger. They can attack, but I'll only disappear; I won't die. It's already been five seconds since B vanished. The fact that I'm still okay means they haven't realized I'm an assassin yet.*

C touched the photon gun hidden inside his jacket.

It's okay. I can get it done.

He let out a deep breath and waited for the Hokage to pass in front of him. Just a little longer. A few more steps.

Then he noticed a man with black hair standing on the other side of the path created by the red carpet. Being a head taller than anyone around him, he was quite conspicuous. While everyone else was focused on the Hokage, he alone was sweeping his gaze out across the citizens instead of looking at the hero from the Land of Fire. His chiseled features were only too well known among the shinobi.

Uchiha Sasuke. Even that monster was part of the guard?

A frontal attack was out of the question, C decided and pulled a nearby woman to him.

"Don't move! I'll kill her!" he shouted, pressing the barrel of the gun to the woman's forehead. People around them shrieked and scattered. Sasuke stepped out to protect the Hokage, who had now stopped walking.

Perfect. The photon gun had enough firepower to pierce seven grown men standing in a line. He would get rid of both of them in one go!

The man raised his arm to turn the barrel toward Sasuke's chest. At least, that's what he intended to do. But somehow, it wasn't his arm that moved but his finger. His lightly bent middle finger moved on its own and pulled the trigger.

The laser shot out of the barrel and through the woman's temple.

Bang!

Flying out from inside her shattered head were...crows. Too many to count.

"Huh?"

Ebony feathers danced up around him.

He was suddenly overcome by a dizzying torpor, and unable to stay on his feet, C dropped to his knees.

Genjutsu. He knew it, but he still couldn't fight his eyelids slipping downward.

Poof!

C disappeared.

They got all my doppelgangers.

Yanaru bit his lip.

Hatake Kakashi. Haruno Sakura. And Uchiha Sasuke. The security for the Seventh Hokage was over the top. Given the

Hokage's own strength, it was excessive—no ifs, ands, or buts about it. Yanaru seriously doubted that today's inspection warranted this kind of firepower.

Or maybe the advance intel he'd been given was actually true?

He'd only half listened to the story about the Seventh Hokage being seriously ill, so weak that he was no stronger than the average person in a fight. Yanaru hadn't believed his luck could possibly be that good. Now, however, seeing the body-guards the Hokage was traveling with, it took on the flavor of truth. This crew wouldn't come together unless the situation was that serious.

In which case, this was maybe a once-in-a-lifetime opportunity?

"Lord Hokage." Yanaru stood in the middle of the carpet and looked back at the Hokage walking behind him.

"Hm?" Uzumaki Naruto also stopped and turned his carefree blue eyes toward Yanaru. He looked without suspicion at Yanaru, who had accompanied and guarded him constantly these past three days.

Yanaru swiftly approached the Hokage and moved diago-nally to create a blind spot. He turned the kunai he had hidden in his sleeve toward the Hokage's chest.

The tip hovered above his heart, coated in a deadly poison, and Yanaru was about to push it in when his body abruptly stiffened.

He couldn't move. Not his hands or his feet. He couldn't even blink.

"What a hassle." Naruto sighed in annoyance. "Honestly, making us work like that. You're the last of the assassins, yeah?"

Naruto's palm strike drove into his solar plexus, and Yanaru gasped.

His mind went blank as he toppled forward into Naruto's arms.

"Moegi, Udon. This is the real one. Take him away."

The two young guards on standby behind Naruto quietly stepped forward and held Yanaru up by each arm.

He wanted to tell them to let go, but his throat was frozen and he couldn't speak. He tried to run, but his body would not obey him.

The only part of him that was still functioning properly was his ears. He could hear people cheering. No one in the crowd seemed to have noticed there was a battle unfolding before their very eyes.

Yanaru was dragged away and handed over to the Kizahashi guards.

The Seventh Hokage walked forward, head held high, responding to the applause of the people with his gaze, and stepped up the ramp and into the airship. At the top of the ramp, he looked back at the crowd, and the cheering grew noticeably louder. He locked eyes with a boy jumping up and waving his hand, and waved in return.

Once the airship lifted off, the Hokage moved away from his staff and headed toward the passenger cabin that had been prepared for him. Before he pulled the door open, he felt around for auras in the area, and after confirming he was alone, he slipped into the room.

Lying on the floor in the middle of the cabin was Uzumaki Naruto.

"Nnnn! Mmph hngh ngh! Mgg nph hnnngh!"

His hands and feet were bound, and his mouth was gagged.

"Don't glare at me. And I totally have no idea what you're saying."

The Hokage removed the gag, wet with saliva, and Naruto howled, "Shikamaru! Untie me this second!"

"What else were we supposed to do? You wouldn't listen to us."

"I *told* you I was going to go to today's meeting!"

Poof!

The usual sound was heard as Shikamaru shed the look of the Hokage he had worn to the meeting and returned to his original appearance. He scratched his head in annoyance.

"They basically agreed to everything we wanted. The import price of gas will be the same, no increase. I don't know if that's why, but there were assassins in the mix, looking to take you out. My taking your place was definitely the right choice."

"What?" The look on Naruto's face changed at the word *assassins*. "No one was hurt, right?"

"Like we'd let anyone get hurt. Who do you think was standing guard?" Shikamaru said coolly as he untied Naruto.

The ropes were reinforced with the full force of the scientific ninja tool team and imbued with concentrated chakra. They couldn't be ripped apart with the strength Naruto currently possessed.

"The assassin was a four-person cell made up of three shadow doppelgangers and himself. The doppelgangers were all taken care of by the guards. The man himself I caught with Shadow Possession, and we handed him over to the Kizahashi side. I hope they get him to spill who hired him."

"So the guards... No way."

Naruto had a sudden bad feeling about all of this, and as if in response, a board on the ceiling was peeled away to allow three figures to drop down soundlessly. Hatake Kakashi, Uchiha Sakura, and Uchiha Sasuke—the team guarding the Seventh Hokage that day.

Naruto looked at each of them in turn and then lowered his eyes in frustration. "I told you. I don't need bodyguards."

He hated this so much.

If only he wasn't in the state he was in, he wouldn't need to waste shinobi this powerful on babysitting the Hokage.

Chapter 1

The first episode had occurred six months earlier.

He was pretty sure it was his second night of no sleep in a streak of all-nighters—maybe even the third. He'd had new ordinances to enact and a meeting of the Five Kages all in the same week. It was a busy time. He hadn't been feeling well for a few days. He was dazed, sluggish, and maybe running a slight fever, but above all else, he wasn't sleeping, so he figured he was just out of sorts from sleep deprivation.

"Naruto, sorry. Could you give us another doppelganger?"

It was after two in the morning when Shikamaru came into the Hokage's office, deep, dark circles under his eyes.

"The institute made some last-minute progress with the chakra research," he said wearily. "That in and of itself is great, but now the numbers for the meeting have changed, and we basically need to redo all the documents. And we do *not* have enough people to do it."

"Yeah," Naruto answered just as wearily and lifted his face from his computer.

His eyes were tired and dry from glaring at numbers in a

spreadsheet. He leaned back in his chair, rubbed his eyes, and blinked repeatedly before weaving signs without thinking about much of anything. Just like always.

Instantly, an intense bolt of pain shot through his chest, like his torso was being ripped in two.

"Aaah?!" He fell forward, his head hit his desk, and he dropped to his knees on the floor.

"Naruto?!" Shikamaru cried.

After a second or two, the pain disappeared like a wave receding, and all that was left were the tingling aftershocks.

"What's wrong, Naruto? What hurts?" Shikamaru peered at him, brow furrowed.

"Oh. For a second there, my chest, it was like..." Naruto staggered to his feet.

What *was* that? He'd never experienced that kind of pain before. Was it because he was weaving signs?

Nervously, he locked his fingers together once more.

Poof!

A doppelganger appeared.

"Huh." He stared at it. "There it is."

"What just happened there?" Shikamaru asked.

"Yeah, it was like, I dunno, this serious pain was like, *shrr-rmp*." Naruto described the pain with a noise that didn't sound particularly painful.

"High blood pressure?" his doppelganger teased, patting him on the shoulder. "It's 'cause all you eat is ramen."

"Shut up!" Naruto snapped. "I'm not *that* old, you know!"

"..."

Shikamaru watched the two carry on with a hard look on his face. He was aware that the burden on the Hokage was too great with the current administrative system. He'd submitted proposal after proposal to the daimyo to revise and improve the system, but resistance to change was strong because it meant going against tradition. Any debate over these proposals had been postponed time and again since it was not considered an urgent matter.

Naruto had been pushing himself too hard for way too long.

And yet, Shikamaru couldn't just tell him to take some time off. But watching him struggle was hard to bear. Theoretically, the Hokage was the leader of the institution responsible for defending the Land of Fire, the shinobi village. But during the long years of endless war, the entire nation had come to depend on the shinobi for more than just defense and looked to them for community leadership. The authority of the Hokage consequently grew in proportion, beyond the bounds of defense. The Hokage became the leader of the military force of the shinobi village, but he also supervised administrative matters. It was a complex and delicate position that required disciplined discretion of the individual himself. And so it was hard to simply redistribute some of the Hokage tasks.

"This won't make you feel better, but drink it anyway." Shikamaru tossed Naruto some herbal medicine mixed up by the medical team.

Naruto drank down the energy drink, got himself back on track, and focused on his duties, and before long, he had completely forgotten the flash of lightning that had raced through his chest.

The second time the pain came was two weeks later.

He was out on the training ground with his son, Boruto, one evening. The meeting of the Five Kages had ended without incident, and he was watching Boruto train to make up for time he hadn't spent with his son in a while.

"Ha! Ho! Da! Hiyah!"

The shuriken that Boruto launched one after the other spun neatly through the air and struck the targets to the north, east, south, and west. *Thok! Thok! Thok! Thok!*

He was doing shuriken and kunai throwing practice, his worst skills.

"Yesssss! I got 'em!" he cried.

"Whoa, nice work," Naruto said. "Okay, next we'll practice an even tighter curve."

"What? Tighter than that? I want to practice Rasengan though." Boruto looked back at Naruto reproachfully and sulked. "I mean, I got Sarada on my team, y'know? I can just let her do the shuriken stuff."

"Listen, you." Naruto looked down at his son. "Once you're a chunin, you won't be teamed up with the same people all the time."

"But, like, I don't know what to do with the curves. Isn't there a trick or something?"

A trick...

Naruto put his hands on his hips and thought about it.

"Right. Can you put a curve on Rasengan?"

"A little," Boruto replied.

"I feel like it's kinda like that."

"Meaning?" Boruto's blue eyes shone with expectation as he looked up at Naruto.

"I told you. When you wanna bend the Rasengan, you go like—" Naruto suddenly stopped. This was an action he performed through feel and instinct, like how he moved his arms and legs. He tried to articulate the process in words, but he couldn't find the right words.

"You gotta go *gah*, and then *bam*. You know." He himself was aware that his words conveyed no meaning.

But surprisingly, Boruto nodded. "Ohh, I get it. Go *gah*, and then *bam*. Huh. Like that, okay."

Definitely my kid.

Naruto was tickled and tousled Boruto's spiky blonde hair.

"Huh? Quit it!" Boruto swung back and forth and shrugged

his shoulders to evade Naruto's hand, but for all his annoyed gesturing, he seemed pretty happy. "Okay. Practice start. You make some obstacles with Earth Style, Dad, and I'll avoid them to hit the targets."

"Yeah, yeah."

Boruto turned his back to Naruto and readied his shuriken.

Naruto brought his hands together. Just like he always did, he went to weave signs and knead his chakra.

Thump!

Suddenly, his heart pounded hard. A familiar dizzying pain spread out in his chest.

"Nnnngh!" On the verge of screaming, Naruto gritted his teeth. He pressed a hand to his chest and let out a long breath. With his back turned to his father, Boruto hadn't noticed anything.

"Boruto... Sorry." Naruto mustered his strength to keep his voice from shaking and worked hard to act like he was fine, that everything was fine. "Looks like your dad...has an emergency to take care of."

"Whaaat? *Again*?" Boruto said unhappily and turned around.

But Naruto was already kicking at the ground. *Hyoo!* He left so fast, it looked like he had simply vanished.

The ground was ringed with woods for training purposes, and now Naruto raced through those trees, hurrying toward the old city.

His heart was thumping and pounding faster and faster. This was not normal. He had to get to the hospital—get Sakura to take a look at him.

Thump!

Electric agony drilled into his body, and Naruto flipped over and collapsed on the spot. He dug his nails into the earth and somehow managed to sit up, but he couldn't find the strength to do anything more than stay slumped over.

"Ngh!"

It was no use. There was no way he could make it to the hospital. Desperately, he crawled forward and managed to make his way into an aviary in the woods.

It had been built a long time ago to raise falcons for communication purposes and was still in use at the time of the Great War, but it had sat empty for several years now. The walls, exposed to the wind and the rain, were on the verge of crumbling. Screws flew out of the chicken wire when Naruto pushed against it, and it tumbled with him into the small building.

"Haah... Ngh... Ugh..."

The inside of the aviary was also in a sorry state. Old feathers stained with rainwater strewn across the floor emitted a rank smell. Naruto pulled himself on all fours across the rotten sawdust that covered the ground and curled up in one corner.

No matter what, he couldn't let the people of the village see him like this. Not this sniveling, pathetic version of the Seventh Hokage who was supposed to protect the village. It would only cause worry.

"Ngh. Ah, ah, aaah!"

Waves of pain washed through his body, so intense that he could hardly breathe. He couldn't stop the shaking that came up from deep in his core.

"Ngh... Unh. Unnnh!"

How long was he there like that, covered in mud?

Naruto leaned back against the wall and looked up at the ceiling with boards missing. He took a deep breath.

When the pain finally subsided, his face was covered in tears and sweat and saliva.

"I didn't get to finish Boruto's lesson."

He was talking to himself, but a voice inside his head answered. *This is not the time to be bothered about that.*

"Huh, Kurama?" he said, surprised. "You're awake?"

When my vessel moans and groans so dramatically, it does tend to wake me up.

Despite his usual post-awakening grumpiness, Kurama's voice was clear.

I was convinced you were under attack. Naruto, what happened?

"No idea." He wiped his face with his sleeve, pressed a hand to the wall, and got to his feet. "I tried to weave a sign, and my chest suddenly started hurting."

A sign?

"Yeah. Last time too. The second I went to weave a sign."

Naruto. Kurama's voice grew even more serious. *If you wish to be free of regret, assemble trustworthy comrades and begin to investigate immediately.*

"Investigate?"

Yes, Kurama continued slowly. *When the old Sage was staying in the Land of Redaku, he had the same symptoms. He managed to recover somehow. But, Naruto, I don't know if that will be the case for you as well.*

•

Outside of the traditional sweets shop in the old city, there was a sign that said, "Strawberry daifuku are finished for today."

Tami, the owner of the shop, was sitting on the bench outside, wearing the same cherry-pink jacket her staff wore. The enormous bun on the top of her head was quite conspicuous.

"Lord Hokage." She stood up thoughtfully when she noticed Naruto and turned a smile on him.

"Hey, Tami!" he said. "Closing early?"

"We did good business again today. It's getting to be time I opened a second shop."

"I wish you would. My son was grumbling about how your daifuku are impossible to get."

Tami laughed and turned her gaze toward the shop. "They're all here. You're the last to arrive."

"Got it." Naruto opened the door with familiar ease. The showcase at the front of the shop was modern glass paneling, but one step inside revealed a wooden house in the old style. An account book and abacus stood on the shelf of the narrow reception area. A mosquito coil smoldered in one corner of the room, and the thin stream of smoke slipped up and escaped outside through gaps in the transom.

Naruto took off his shoes and stepped up into the room. He pulled the hair ornament used as a bookmark out of the account book and inserted one of the dangling cherry branch decorations into a small hole in the wall.

Vwwm.

A motor hummed, and a lock snapped open.

The wall appeared to be made of a reddish-brown wood, but now it was suddenly transparent like a sheet of acrylic.

This was a Kengakuin research institute invention that used liquid crystal to transform a transparent material into a pattern using the application of a current. The device could perfectly reproduce any kind of material right down to the texture, so it was handy for hiding large objects and entrances to rooms.

Naruto pushed on the wall, and it turned like a revolving door, allowing him inside.

Up ahead was a hidden room.

When Pain attacked Konohagakure, the shop owner Tami hadn't been able to flee in time, and Sakura had rescued her. She had been very devoted to Sakura and their relationship ever since. That same devotion led to the hidden room at Tami Sweets as the venue for this meeting of Naruto and his friends.

Tami likely hadn't the slightest idea that the Seventh Hokage was facing a real crisis. She knew that Naruto and his friends were famous and figured they were looking for a private place to hang out together away from prying eyes.

Naruto made his way up the narrow staircase, and when he pushed open the sliding door at the end of a short hallway, a lantern's light flickered across the bare beams of the small attic room.

Kakashi, Sasuke, Sakura, and Shikamaru were all sitting around a small fire.

Naruto reached behind himself to pull the door shut and sat down cross-legged on the tatami mats. Sweets and tea were set out on top of a round lacquered tray, perhaps a thoughtful gesture from Tami.

"How are you feeling?" The first to open her mouth was Sakura, as she turned concerned eyes on him.

"Mm. Well, about the same," he said.

"Meaning it's not any better, hm? How many episodes have you had since we got back from the Land of Kizahashi?" she asked.

"..."

"Be honest."

Sensing the sharp edge in Sakura's voice, Naruto replied reluctantly, "Two. One big, one little."

"I see." Sakura's voice was cool. He could tell she was trying not to let on how serious she felt it was.

The intense pain in his chest, the trouble breathing—the first two attacks had been when he kneaded his chakra, but ever since the third one, they'd been happening out of the blue when he was doing nothing at all. And they were increasing in frequency. The cause was unknown. Sakura had examined him, but she hadn't found anything out of the ordinary. She'd also been unable to find any bacterial or viral infection, so there was no treatment for him. All she could do was tell him not to use chakra.

The only insight they had about his affliction was that the Sage of Six Paths had it too. According to Nine Tails, the Sage of Six Paths had also suffered from the exact same symptoms that now troubled Naruto.

This was back when the old Sage had just let Ten Tails into his body. He'd had episodes of pain and apparently recovered when he was staying in the remote Land of Redaku in the west. They just didn't know *how* he'd gotten better.

"Maybe you should talk to Hinata about your symptoms," Sakura suggested.

Naruto shook his head. He didn't want to worry his family unnecessarily.

"Let's get right to it. I've got a progress report," Shikamaru calmly interjected. "We've gone through all the libraries in the land, looking for anything on the Land of Redaku, but to be honest, we've got nothing. The very existence of the Land of Redaku is treated like a legend in most books, and I can't find anything with any details. About the only one that looks to be of any help at all is this."

Shikamaru tossed a bundle of papers onto the tatami. A copy of the book in question.

"Unfortunately, it's written in an ancient language, so we won't be reading it anytime soon. But I managed to pick out the proper nouns and can confirm that there's stuff about when the Sage of Six Paths was in the Land of Redaku. That's about all I can get from it. I've asked the institute to decipher it, but I expect it'll take them some time."

The Kengakuin research institute was the international agency built with the consensus of the Five Great Nations after the Great Ninja War. Unlike the village's scientific team, the agency did not belong to any nation in particular. Its purpose was to forward the development of science, culture, and education. Its head office was currently located in the Land of Kizahashi.

"Not great, hm?" Kakashi said and continued without urgency as he poured tea into cups. "You're not the only one with nothing. I sent a hawk to the king of the Land of Redaku and asked about the Sage of Six Paths' stay there. But I got no reply. Maybe something happened."

The Land of Redaku, separated from the outside world by a mountain range thirteen thousand feet high, had maintained a policy of strict isolation for so many centuries that it now belonged to an entirely different cultural sphere than the Land of Fire and the other Great Nations. In recent years, as Hokage, Kakashi had started corresponding with Redaku's king, the first official exchange between the two countries in recorded history. The letters were nothing more than a simple exchange of information about their respective nations, and it was more a modest correspondence between two leaders rather than any kind of diplomatic relations.

The way things stood, Naruto and his friends simply had too little information to go on.

"Looks like our only option is actually to go there ourselves," Sasuke said, sounding totally sedate as usual. Directly ahead of him, the round firelight of the lamp flickered and filled the room.

I'll go.

Naruto somehow managed to swallow the words on the tip of his tongue. They had no idea how many days it was to the Land of Redaku. The Seventh Hokage couldn't exactly disappear for a lengthy period on unofficial business.

"I'll go." It was Kakashi who offered himself up. "I'm the only one here who has a connection with Redaku's king. I wanted to go and see him sometime after I retired anyway, so this is perfect. Plus, I've got nothing going on right now."

"Even if you take the train to the far west of the Five Great Nations and then go to the capital from there," Sakura said, "if you hurry, it'll take maybe two weeks?"

"No." Sasuke shook his head. "He'll need to get his body used to the oxygen concentration at higher altitudes. It'll take twenty days."

"Right." Kakashi nodded. "Well, either way, best to leave as soon as possible, hm?"

"Master Kakashi, you don't have to do this." Naruto threw cold water on the conversation unfolding before him.

Shikamaru turned exasperated eyes on him. "Of course he does. You can't keep going like this."

"But this is my own personal problem. Master Kakashi... Sasuke, Sakura, Shikamaru, you're all valuable resources for Konoha. I can't go using you for something like this."

Sasuke glared questioningly at Naruto. "Those who don't obey will be stripped of ninja status?" he said, obvious anger in his voice.

Naruto fell silent.

Kakashi quickly spoke up again. "That's exactly right. We're ninja failures, Naruto, when it comes to you. Sorry I can't live up to your expectations, but when something's going on with you, I just can't make myself care about going by the books."

Naruto slowly lifted his gaze and looked at each of his friends in turn. None of them showed it on their faces, but he had known them all a long time, so he could tell just how worried they were. Kurama had told him to get his friends together to investigate the illness, and the first people he had spoken to were these four.

But the truth was, he hadn't wanted to tell anyone. He didn't want to cause any extra worry over him.

"Well, I get how you feel." Kakashi shifted his weight where he sat cross-legged. "But whatever you say, I'm going to the Land of Redaku. If I'm going, though, it'd be a huge help if we could make it official Hokage business, rather than private business. I could use the travel budget."

Travel expenses were not the real reason for this request.

Naruto glared at the tatami mats. If the media found out about Kakashi's trip to the Land of Redaku after the fact, they would probably tear Naruto apart: "The Hokage is using the shinobi of the village for personal business." But if there was a record of it being an official mission, then at least he couldn't be criticized for a private dispatch.

"Naruto," Shikamaru said, and Naruto lifted his gaze. "If I can speak as the Hokage's aide, we shouldn't begrudge the resources in looking for a reason for this illness. If something happened to you, it would be a devastating loss for the village. To be honest, it would have an impact on the power balance of the Five Great Nations."

"And we also bear responsibility for bringing this on." Kakashi picked up where Shikamaru left off. "We've relied on you too much for too long. Both during the Fourth Great Ninja War and the rebuilding afterward. The daimyo of the other countries acknowledge that your strength is what built the peace we have now, and you've also been a major part of building up the Land of Fire. But the end result's been all the heavy burdens being placed on your shoulders alone."

"That's..."

I mean, it's the same for you guys.

Naruto looked around at his friends.

Shikamaru, supporting the Hokage both onstage and behind the scenes as his adviser; Sasuke, protecting Konoha from the shadows in his missions in undeveloped areas; Sakura, giving her everything to developing medical treatments; Kakashi, who laid the foundations for the current Konoha as the Sixth Hokage—although their roles were all different, they were all shouldering the same burden.

"I'll go too," Sasuke declared abruptly. "The Land of Redaku's a city-state. Information may not necessarily be concentrated in the capital. Better to have more hands on deck."

"No, Sasuke," Naruto said. "I can't go using you for my illness. Absolutely not."

They already had a very capable resource in the form of Kakashi on the job. Naruto couldn't also involve Sasuke in what was his own personal problem.

"Sasuke. I need you on other missions for the sake of the village. That's... That is very much an order as Hokage."

"But I don't have to obey it," Sasuke told him. "I'm not an official shinobi. I work with you because I want to."

"Don't give me that!" A vein popped up on Naruto's forehead. "Which is more important—the future of the village or my life?!"

"Your life," came Sasuke's immediate response. "Without it, we can't protect the future of the village. Whatever you say, I'm going to do what I think is best."

"Anyone want tea?" Sakura held up the teapot to interrupt their bickering.

"Please." Shikamaru put his cup forward.

Kakashi followed suit. "I'll have some too."

Pale green liquid spilled gently from the spout and swirled around as it filled the insides of the teacups.

"..."

Naruto narrowed his eyes sharply like a fox and glared at Sasuke. Not to be outdone, Sasuke glared back with an equally powerful stare.

"Okay, I'll go to the Land of Redaku first and poke around," Kakashi said slowly, holding his steaming cup of tea in both hands. "If I need help, I'll send a hawk. It won't be too late for Sasuke to come then."

"Right." Sakura nodded and reached for a strawberry daifuku. "Sasuke, you can watch Sarada and Boruto train for the first time in a while."

Neither Naruto nor Sasuke said anything, but simply continued to glare at each other in the small space lit with the wavering fire.

Shikamaru let out an annoyed sigh.

The next morning, after getting the Seventh Hokage's seal on his papers for an out-of-country mission, Kakashi set off for the Land of Redaku.

Naruto was too busy—and too frustrated by his illness of unknown cause—to wallow in guilt for dispatching Kakashi. Between attending various meetings in multiple locations, he also finished off the mountain of paperwork on his desk. In the afternoon, he received a report on the Anbu's investigations, followed by a discussion of how to address the suspicious movements of international agencies. Should their response be urgent? Should they act even without concrete proof? The meeting took them into the evening, and though it was heated, they eventually settled on maintaining the status quo and remaining vigilant. By the time Naruto returned to his office, the sun had long set. As he began his slow review of proposals for the new curriculum at the academy he sucked down a tube of nutrient jelly instead of eating actual food. Then Shikamaru walked in.

"You're still here?" he said casually, an open laptop computer resting on one arm. "Any episodes today?"

"Not a one," Naruto replied.

The truth was, there had been one, just this afternoon. Fortunately, he'd been alone in his office, and it wasn't too severe, so he'd locked the door and waited for it to pass while he curled into himself.

"Yeah?" Shikamaru closed the door behind him. "Rejoice, Naruto. I got a note from the institute. Said they're making progress deciphering that text."

"For real?!" Naruto leaped to his feet.

"Shizune joining the deciphering team's been huge. Shock and awe. They've gotten four whole lines in a single day."

"Gre—"

Four lines? That's it?

"Okay, you don't need to be so obviously disappointed," Shikamaru said. "Those four lines had a ton of info in them. When he visited the Land of Redaku, the Sage of Six Paths apparently stayed at the astronomical observatory opened by this astronomer called Jean-Marc Tatar. There's a real possibility that he recovered from his illness while he was there."

"Whoa! And?"

"And? That's it."

"Come on..." Shoulders slumping, Naruto dropped back down into his chair. "Well. That is a step forward at least!" He forced a smile onto his face.

"Yup. A step. It might feel small, but you should be happy about it." Shikamaru pulled a nearby garbage can toward him, spread his legs, and sat down. "I sent a hawk to let Master Kakashi know. Although we should still have him head for the capital first, like we planned. And then...about the assassination attempt in the Land of Kizahashi. It seems the would-be assassin Aze Yanaru killed himself."

Naruto scowled at this.

"In the end, we didn't get any intel from him about who was behind it," Shikamaru continued with a hard look on his face. He tapped at the laptop to bring up an email. "The Land of Kizahashi investigation team sent a list of questions for the Seventh Hokage. Stuff like, 'Do you have any enemies?'"

"Whaaat? I've got way too many of those, believe it."

"Right."

As the Hokage, Naruto was in a position which made it inevitable that he would have at least a few enemies. As the peace continued and memories of the Great Ninja War faded from hearts and minds, there were people, even among the villagers of Konoha, who spoke venomously behind his back, saying things like "A hero of war is basically a murderer."

"The fact that he deliberately targeted you at that meeting might mean someone from Kizahashi was involved," Shikamaru said, frowning in annoyance. "There are sparks flying between the two countries over the price of gas, right?"

"So it's about Kizahashi gas?" Naruto asked, arching an eyebrow.

"The folks in Kizahashi don't like how the institute is developing new energy sources with Land of Fire funding. They won't be able to keep going if demand for their gas drops."

Naruto frowned.

It was true that the Land of Kizahashi had sent a number of petitions (read: pressure) to put a stop to the development of new energy sources. The reason given was that it would "disrupt the current economic balance." But markets naturally fluctuated, so this was a ridiculous "reason."

It wasn't as though Naruto wanted to diminish the economic power of the Land of Kizahashi. But the Land of Fire couldn't depend on other countries for energy forever.

"The director of the institute's looking pretty sketchy. Some people are wondering if he wasn't the ringleader behind the assassination attempt."

Shikamaru launched a web browser and brought up the institute's official homepage. A photo of the director was on the page introducing the organization. He looked high-strung and wore glasses.

"Kanhen Furieh. Director of the institute and physicist specializing in energy. He was born in the Land of Kizahashi and studied in the Land of Fire as a special student during the time of the Sixth Hokage."

"Meaning he could come study in the Land of Fire because Master Kakashi put up the money," Naruto said. "So then why would he have a grudge against us?"

"It's possible his love for his country might be stronger than his debt to us," Shikamaru replied, tapping his laptop's keyboard. The screen switched to a list of shinobi affiliated with the village of Konohagakure. "Don't know if Furieh's in it, but at any rate, it's a fact that the assassination was planned. Probably a good idea to send a team to the Land of Kizahashi to investigate. It's too difficult a mission to give to a genin, so I was thinking we put together a team with Konohamaru and Mira, a couple others—"

"No," Naruto said firmly. "Send Sasuke."

"You sure?" Shikamaru raised his eyebrows.

"Yeah." He nodded. "As long as Sasuke's here, he'll tend to me and this sickness. But I need him working for the sake of the village. No one else can do what he does."

"If that's your decision, fine. Are you going to notify him about it?"

"No. You tell him, Shikamaru. Like always."

As if waiting for this break in their conversation, someone knocked at the door.

Without waiting for a reply, Moegi poked her head in and called to Shikamaru. There was a message from the institute.

"I get it, Naruto. I'll tell Sasuke," Shikamaru said, and then left the Hokage's office.

In the end, Naruto didn't leave the office until the late evening turned into the wee hours of an early tomorrow.

"Aah.... I'm wiped."

The mere touch of the night breeze on his skin felt rejuvenating, which also revealed how exhausted he was. The world in darkness was a soothing balm to his eyes, which had been staring into the glare of a computer screen all night.

He dragged his feet through the old city, and seven faces abruptly popped into view on the other side of the power lines.

Hokage Rock.

He hadn't been up there in a while, and he was seized with the sudden urge to see the view from the top of the rock again. So he whirled around and changed direction. He couldn't use chakra, so he scrambled up the rock using his hands, sat on the stone face of his father, and looked out on the old city.

A sparse night scene dotted with the lights of houses here and there.

This modest sight was Naruto's pride. Beneath each and every one of those gentle lights was a person, and it made him happy to think about them eating supper or taking a bath with hard-fought security. This village was at peace. No one feared an invasion or attack from another nation, there was no threat of food scarcity, and there was no fear that a father who left home on a mission wouldn't come home again. In this tranquility, Master Kakashi laughed and told him old stories about Obito and Team Minato, and Sasuke took Sakura and Sarada to visit the graves of his family. Even as they carried their sad memories with them, they continued to move forward bit by bit.

He wished he could have shown this world to his mom and dad. And to the Pervy Sage. And Pain. And Neji. And Zabuza and Haku. To think that the village of Konoha could be this peaceful.

The truth was, he wanted all of them in this world too. How amazing it would have been for all of them to smile at each other and say, "We're so lucky we get to live together in peace."

He wished they were all still alive. He'd had enough of people suffering and dying. Naruto wanted to bring peace to the village. That was why he'd set out to become Hokage.

The one who is accepted by all becomes the Hokage—Naruto had always worked for the sake of everyone else but himself. He wasn't so great at having anyone do anything for him.

But whenever anyone was watching his back, they were Naruto's shield.

"..."

Naruto stood up and looked down at the nose of the Fourth, a little higher up on the face than was his own. At some point, he had gotten older than Minato was the day he was killed in the line of duty. Even now that his dream of being the Hokage had come true, Naruto's ninja path was unchanged.

To never twist his own words.

To keep fulfilling his dream of protecting the village as Hokage.

But to do so, he had to be strong.

"I really gotta do something about this." He tried talking to himself, but even he could tell his voice was lacking spirit.

Pushing away this anxiety, he clenched his hands into fists. At the same time, he dropped to his knees.

An electrical current shot through his chest. His heart started to pound faster, and fireworks bounced around in his skull.

"Ngh... Ungh. Ah! ...Haah!"

Intense pain shot through his body. This time it felt deeper than usual.

"Why... ah. Ngh... It's not...the same—"

His limbs trembled, and his body spasmed. The moisture of his throat evaporated.

On all fours, Naruto moaned and clenched his teeth.

His consciousness threatened to exit his head, but the pain pulsing through his body quickly brought it back.

Be calm. It's the same as always. Grit your teeth and it'll be over before you know it.

No sooner had he told himself this than a new level of extreme pain electrified his body to its core.

"Aunh?!" He flapped his mouth open and closed and sent up a silent scream.

His pulse was wild, his heart leaped erratically in his chest, and his body was so hot, it threatened to catch fire.

"Ngh! Hngh. Ah. Aah!"

The heat and intense pain were practically ripping him open from the inside.

"Ah! Aunh. Aunnnhhh!"

He lost consciousness and slid down from the rocky face of the Fourth Hokage. His body seized and shuddered, and as he fell he was caught by someone's arms.

Naruto felt the soft *thud* of a landing, and the consciousness that had left him returned.

Through a haze he saw familiar feet encased up to the ankle in traditional *tabi* shoes.

"Sasuke..."

Sasuke had Naruto tucked under his arm and gently set him down on the ground. He was kneading chakra in the palm of his hand. He created Water Style water and spilled it onto Naruto's face, cooling the fire inside of Naruto's head, which was on the verge of overheating.

Sasuke started to walk away.

From the sound of his footsteps, Naruto realized that Sasuke was moving in the opposite direction of his house. Naruto pulled himself into a sitting position.

"Hold up, Sasuke..."

He desperately squinted to try and clear his foggy vision.

The receding Sasuke was wearing the long black coat with a collar that he always wore on missions. From the unnatural bulge of it, Naruto knew he had a longsword on his back.

"You... What's with that outfit? You going somewhere?"

Sasuke stopped and looked back. "As you can see, I'm leaving Konoha."

"You going to the astronomical observatory?"

Sasuke nodded evenly.

The blood rose to Naruto's freshly cooled head again. "C'mon, man... You got a notice from Shikamaru. Your next mission is to investigate who was behind the assassination attempt in the Land of Kizahashi. You can't just go off—"

"Not my problem," Sasuke said coolly and turned a strong, even angry gaze on Naruto. "If you're not the Hokage, then there's no point. I won't go on any other missions until you're cured."

"You... Not happening, Sasuke." Naruto put some strength into his buckling knees and desperately pushed himself to his feet. Once Sasuke made up his mind, he never changed it. If Naruto was going to stop him, it would have to be with force.

He kneaded chakra in the loose palm of his left hand.

Instantly, a jolt of pain shot through his spine, and he nearly leaped into the air.

Stop, Naruto! He heard Kurama say.

Shut up, he replied in his head and continued to knead his chakra.

The chakra was imbued with wind and began to spin chaotically.

As if in response, Sasuke concentrated chakra in his right hand. Visible voltage bounced up, and the high-pitched cry of Chidori rang out.

While pain shredded every part of him, Naruto readied his Rasengan and started running. Sasuke prepared to counter, raising his right hand to launch Chidori.

Thump!

Naruto staggered in agony. His reflexes gave up on releasing chakra. His Rasengan instantly faded away. And Sasuke's Chidori flew at Naruto's chest as he started to pitch forward.

The pale electrical attack pierced his chest.

"Aungh!"

Naruto dropped to his knees and was about to press a hand to his stomach where he'd been shot through, but he couldn't find any wound.

When he looked up, Sasuke was looking down at him coolly from a distance.

Genjutsu? he thought as he toppled over. Perhaps his forcible kneading of chakra left him with zero strength. Even still, he managed to grasp at the earth and brace himself, but after thrusting his arms out and pushing his upper body up, he collapsed back onto the ground.

"Going easy on me," Naruto squeezed out, while he ate dirt. "Going easy on a rival."

"Because you're a rival," Sasuke replied and turned his back to Naruto, the hem of his long coat swinging. "Naruto. Do not die before I get back."

"I'm telling you not to go..."

The sound of Sasuke's footsteps faded. He was headed to the astronomical observatory.

"Don't go. Don't go. Don't go," Naruto murmured over and over as he looked up at the muddy night sky. Gradually, he lost even his voice, and all he could make was a faint whistling sound in his throat.

He was so cowardly letting Sasuke go, he could hardly stand it. As the Hokage, he was supposed to protect the village. But here he was now, being protected by people who should have been protecting the village.

"Naruto."

He heard a familiar voice and slowly lifted his eyelids.

Clear green eyes looked down on him in utter exasperation. "Same old idiot as always."

"Me? Sasuke?"

"Both of you, obviously."

Sakura crouched down and gently helped Naruto sit up.
She touched his cheek and poured chakra into the scrapes he'd
gotten falling from the Rock to heal them. Ever since his symptoms had begun, Naruto's natural healing power had dropped
dramatically. Before this, scratches like these would have healed
easily on their own.

"Sasuke left," Naruto said slowly.

Sakura nodded easily. "I know."

"If you know then...why didn't you stop him?"

"I tried. But you know that Sasuke's impossible once he
makes up his mind about something. Now that he's decided
to help you, he'll do everything he can." Sakura removed the
headband she had pushed high on her head to keep her hair
back and set it down in the middle of her forehead as if to cover
the hyakugo jutsu mark there. "I'm going after him soon myself.
He'll probably use Susano'o, though, so I won't be able to catch
up for a while."

"But what about Sarada?" Naruto asked.

"I'll have someone I can trust take her," Sakura said.
"Shizune joined the deciphering team at the institute, so she's not
around. But I'll find someone Sasuke trusts too. Can you stand?"

She slipped herself under Naruto's arm and stood him up,
leaning him on her shoulder. Together, they took one step after
another toward the old city.

"So, listen," Sakura started casually as she matched Naruto's
pace. "You remember you came to the hospital and we did those
detailed tests? I just got the results back. You're basically in
perfect health, but there was one weird thing. It looks like your
chakra channels are closing up."

"My chakra channels?"

Sakura nodded and continued.

"But you don't have pain when I pour my chakra into you, and your scratches did in fact heal, right? That would mean you're not rejecting chakra itself. Most likely, the problem is with your chakra channels. If the Sage of Six Paths had the same symptoms, then the failure of your chakra channels is likely due to taking a Biju into your body."

"But Gaara and Bee and them are all just fine," he protested.

"True," she agreed. "This is just a hypothesis at best."

Naruto lowered his gaze. "If my chakra channels close, what'll happen to me?"

"If the issue is only your chakra channels, you won't die if they close up," Sakura told him. "You just won't ever be able to use chakra again."

"'Just'..." The color drained from Naruto's already ghostly pale face.

With the chakra of the Nine Tails inside of him, Naruto's fighting style depended on the amount of his intrinsic chakra. Not being able to knead chakra now after all this time—to be honest, it would be a fate worse than death.

"That's serious," he said slowly.

"It is," Sakura replied with a sigh. "But I'm relieved at any rate. We're not at war right now, and it doesn't really matter if the Hokage stops being able to use chakra."

She was maybe right about that. But for Naruto, who had dreamed of becoming the Hokage since he was a child, a totally obvious prerequisite was that he had to be strong. That prerequisite hadn't changed since he became the Seventh Hokage.

"..."

Unable to say anything more, Naruto quietly dragged his still-spasming left leg forward.

•

He couldn't go home in his muddied clothes, so he spent the night in the nap room next to his office.

He tossed his filthy clothes into the laundry, curled up in his shorts on the thin futon, and spent the rest of the night in thought.

If he ultimately couldn't use chakra anymore, would he quit as Hokage? Or would he rethink old notions and determine that strength and force in a time of peace were no longer necessary? Would he then remain in his position?

"Aaaaah, I hate both options."

There were still plenty of things he wanted to accomplish as Hokage. He had no interest in passing the torch when there was still more on his to-do list.

Before he knew it, the dawning of a new day came without his getting a wink of sleep. He stepped back into his office early and finished up his routine duties. Not until it was past noon was he finally able to go back to his own house.

When he opened the front door, he found a pair of unfamiliar zori sandals, heels together, neatly placed on the entryway floor.

Maybe Hinata's? Bit big for her though.

He sat down on the step leading up to the house, and as he took off his shoes, Himawari came flying out of the living room, having heard him come in.

"It's Daddy! You're home!"

"I sure am, Himawari."

"Okay, so, we have a guest. He drew this for me!" She beamed at him and held up the paper in her hands. It was a portrait of Himawari and Hinata drawn in gentle pastel colors. Even Naruto, who knew nothing about art, could tell it was well drawn.

A guest who can draw like this? Who?

Naruto looked toward the door of the living room down the hallway. The faces of Sai and Inojin popped up in his head, but the zori in the entryway were very much a woman's.

"Come to the living room! Come on! He's waiting for you, Daddy!"

"Y-you bet." Yanked along by the hand, Naruto poked his head into the living room and almost choked on his tongue.

"Goodness! You're later than I was expecting."

Sitting at the table and sipping tea was the elusive snake man, shiny black hair hanging to his waist—Orochimaru.

Chapter 2

"Home at last. You're as busy as ever then," Orochimaru said in the same old husky voice and took a silent sip from his teacup.

"Huh... Hunh?" Naruto rubbed his eyes, convinced that he was now seeing ghosts. But the vision before him was, without a doubt, real.

Orochimaru was drinking tea. In the Uzumaki living room.

"Hi, Naruto. Welcome home," Hinata said, smiling at him from where she stood in the dining room. "Orochimaru brought strawberry *zenzai*. It's really delicious. Do you want some?"

"H-Hinata," Naruto stammered. "Orochimaru is in our living room..."

"He is. He arrived a little while ago." Hinata's calm was in contrast to Naruto's panic. "I was surprised to see him too, but he's been a real help, playing so much with Himawari. He said he has something to talk to you about."

Talk? Orochimaru? Me? Were we friendly like that?

Hinata set out some tea and strawberry zenzai for him. "Well, I'm off to pick up some things for supper," she said gently and left the living room.

"Right. Be careful," Naruto murmured and then realized he was still standing, so he tentatively pulled out a chair.

Himawari ran in clutching a pencil crayon and wrapped herself around Orochimaru's legs. "Orocchi! Draw moooore!"

"Maybe later, hm?" he said, looking down at her. "I need to talk with your daddy for a second."

"So what do you want to talk about?" Naruto was still baffled, but he nevertheless straightened up in his seat.

Orochimaru had been quietly minding his own business as of late, so Naruto had let his guard down a bit. But he knew the snake man would happily commit any evil for the sake of his own goals. He wasn't the sort of person to sit leisurely in your living room sipping a cup of tea. Not normally.

"Could you be a little less defensive? I came because I wanted to lend you something." Orochimaru reached a hand into the sleeve of his kimono and dug out from its deep pocket a pair of large goggles.

"What're those?" Naruto asked warily.

"My latest invention. These goggles can give you the ocular jutsu of someone else."

Give? Someone else's ocular jutsu?

Naruto blinked rapidly, confused.

In the last few years, there had been remarkable development in technologies that could separate ninjutsu from their users and store them independently. The pioneer of this advancement was Katasuke, and his key inventions were the scientific ninja tools. But ocular jutsu, based on kekkei genkai, were extremely difficult to reproduce. Common thought was that it was impossible for ocular jutsu to be used by other people with scientific ninja tools.

Naruto took the goggles and stared at them. Grey frame with orange lenses.

"So they're like the scientific ninja tools?" he asked. "An average person with no chakra can use these goggles?"

"Yes. Their performance has no relationship to the wearer's chakra. Earlier, your wife was kind enough to work with me to set them with the Byakugan ability."

"The Byakugan?"

Orochimaru looked at Naruto's surprised face, and his smile had a cruel edge. "However, while the ability is set in the goggles, your wife cannot use her Byakugan. Go ahead and put them on."

No matter how he looked at it, this technology was sketchy. But his curiosity outweighed his suspicions, and so Naruto put on the goggles, keeping an eye on Orochimaru the whole time. All he could see through the glass was a slightly warped living room; his field of view did not change.

"Nothing's happening," he said.

"There's a small lever on the frame," Orochimaru told him. "Pull it."

Here? He tugged hard on the little switch to one side of a lens, and his field of vision flipped like he was looking through a kaleidoscope.

"Ah!"

It wasn't a kaleidoscope. It was the familiar sight of his living room. Except that he could see everything. The sink on the other side of the counter, the designs on the plates and cups in the cupboards, the mosquito behind a cushion on the sofa, the movement of Himawari's hands where she sat on the carpet drawing, each and every one of the pages of the sketchbook, everything.

Unable to keep his eyes open any longer, Naruto pushed the goggles up onto his forehead.

"What is that even?!" he yelped. "I can see so much, but I also can't see anything at all!"

"At first, your brain can't keep up and process everything. Train with them."

"Train?"

Naruto guessed at Orochimaru's intentions and narrowed his eyes sharply. "So that's your little game. You're making me test your prototype."

"I wouldn't lend them to you out of the goodness of my heart," Orochimaru said gracefully.

"Why me?" Naruto took off the goggles and stared at them again. "If you want to test a prototype, you've got Suigetsu and Karin. Why come all the way to my house?"

"Well, put simply..." Orochimaru suddenly stretched his neck out. "You can't use chakra now, yes?"

An icy breath stroked the back of his own neck, and Naruto scowled, not hiding the chill he felt. "How do you know that?"

"Snakes have excellent hearing." The forked tip of his long tongue licked at the back of Naruto's ear.

Recoiling in disgust would only make Orochimaru happy. Naruto kept his arms crossed and his face expressionless. Seeing this, Orochimaru smiled, seemingly pleased.

"Working with me isn't such a bad deal for you," he remarked.

"And if I refuse?"

"I don't think you can."

He was exactly right.

Naruto was reluctant to lend a hand to this man's research, but now that he couldn't manipulate chakra, the goggles were appealing. And to be honest, he'd always wondered what the view was like when Hinata was using her Byakugan ability.

With no clue about what was going on, Himawari trotted over and innocently clapped her hands. "Wow! Orocchi, you can stretch your neck out?! You're like a giraffe, huh!"

"A snake. Snake. Not a giraffe." Orochimaru pulled his neck back in and slowly stood up. "I'll come again," he said and headed for the front door.

Utterly smitten, Himawari trotted after him on small feet. "Orocchi, you'll come over again, right? Next time, I want you to draw my brother's picture."

"Yes, all right." He smiled. "I'll draw whatever you'd like."

As always, Naruto was puzzled by this guy.

Shiny black hair swinging, Orochimaru stepped out the front door, and Naruto watched him go with a strange feeling.

In his hands were the mysterious goggles with the power of the Byakugan. If the goggles allowed a person to master a kekkei genkai and an ocular jutsu on top of that, they would definitely be a powerful weapon.

Naruto, though, would be happy if it could compensate for the handicap of not being able to use chakra.

•

That night, sunk deep in the sofa cushions, Naruto stared at the TV without actually watching what was on. He would never let the kids see him looking so slovenly, but it was just him and Hinata in the living room at the moment, and he allowed himself to be a little lazy. He'd been practicing with the Byakugan goggles ever since Orochimaru left. He hadn't trained that hard in a while, and he was completely wiped out.

"What a shock, though," he muttered. "I mean, *that* guy drinking tea in my living room like any regular person."

"Hee hee! I was definitely surprised when the doorbell rang and I opened the door to find Orochimaru." Hinata handed him a warm mug from where she sat next to him. A café au lait made with freshly ground coffee beans and plenty of honey and milk. With a child's sweet tooth, Naruto really liked drinking it this way. But in the Hokage office he and Shikamaru always raised cups of concentrated black coffee (energy drink added).

"Maybe you were surprised, but you seemed to get along with him just fine," Naruto noted.

"He clearly wasn't hostile," Hinata said. "And he's basically a mom friend. Our kids hang out together, after all."

The Orochimaru, a mom friend...

Naruto cocked his head to one side as he drained his mug, and Hinata gently touched his wrist.

"I think you've gotten skinnier, Naruto. Your chakra's still not up to its usual levels?"

"Oh... No, this is..." he tried to protest.

"You're pushing yourself too hard at work again, hm?"

They lived together under the same roof, so of course Hinata would notice that he was not in the best shape, and it was obvious to her—a Byakugan user—that his chakra had dropped. He had explained his weariness as overwork from the busy season. He didn't want to have an episode in front of his family, so he'd been sequestering himself up at his office lately, not coming home too often. Because of this, Hinata didn't seem to suspect that his actual health was suffering.

"Anyway! I practiced using the Byakugan today with Orochimaru's goggles!" Naruto quickly changed the subject. "It didn't go too well. To be honest, it was super hard. It's incredible you and old man Hiashi and Hanabi are such masters."

Whatever else, there were just too many things to look at. His attention would get caught by something too far back in his field of vision, and he'd trip over things, hit his head on outstretched branches, and give himself a bunch of ugly scratches and bruises.

"Hinataaaa, isn't there some kind of trick to it?" he asked, playing with the hair spilling over her shoulders.

"A trick..." Hinata put a finger to her chin as she considered the question. "You just sort of go like this, and then *bam! Shff!*"

"I don't get iiiiiit!" Naruto threw his head back, and she shrugged and grinned.

"It's hard to explain it in words. I feel like Hanabi could explain it better if you asked—Oh!" Hinata slipped out of Naruto's arms and stood up. "Hang on a second?"

She went upstairs and came back down with a small box. A wicker box woven of cypress and colored with persimmon dye.

"Oh!" Naruto sat up straighter. "Your treasure box! I get to look inside it today?"

"Mm hmm. Special for today."

The wicker box, normally set aside in a corner of the closet, was the treasure chest Hinata had cherished since childhood. She'd shown him what was inside just once before when they were first married. It had been full of memories she'd made with him—ticket stubs from date night movies they'd gone to, wrapping paper and ribbons from presents, leftover yarn from the scarf she knit him at some point.

It had been more than ten years since then.

When she opened the lid of the box that still gleamed with the same luster after all these years, he saw that its contents had noticeably increased. A paulownia-wood box containing the umbilical cords of their two children, the acorn necklace Boruto had made her, a portrait Himawari had drawn. A ticket stub for the live-action teen movie *Make-Out Paradise*, the dotted wrapping paper that had wrapped earrings Naruto picked out—they were all in there.

"Okay, so listen. I'm sure that this will help." Ever so tenderly, Hinata pulled out an old notebook from the depths of the box. All four corners were thoroughly worn away, and the ribbon tying it shut was frayed to the point of snapping.

Naruto flipped through its pages, noting the neat rows of characters. "I feel like I've seen this handwriting before."

"Well, you see." Hinata smiled mischievously. "It's Neji's training log."

"Neji's?"

Right. This was Neji's handwriting.

Instantly in that moment, memories came flooding back to him, like a tap had been turned on. The neat, honor-student cursive, as if perfectly tracing the examples Master Iruka gave them. Neji used to scowl every time he saw Naruto's chicken scratches and say, "Chaotic characters make a chaotic mind."

Naruto dropped his eyes to the page once more. Neji hadn't skipped a single day in this record of training on his own. That's who he was. He was a genius, but he also worked tirelessly and was harder on himself than anyone else. He absolutely refused to compromise.

Sunny

Be careful not to try and grasp all of the chakra flowing through the keirakukei network. More effective instead to turn gaze on whole and predict next chakra movement.

Goal for now is to see through all of Tenten's secret tools.

Rainy

The usual pair was at it again today. The second I take my eyes off them, the teenage drama starts.

Wasn't able to dodge the iron fan Tenten threw, cut my cheek. How to cover the Byakugan's blind spot needs study.

Sunny

Lost in the first fight of final selection.

I don't have that unpredictability he does—the imagination to upend expectations of others.

The notebook was completely yellowed and discolored, but still in surprisingly good condition, considering how many years it had weathered. Proof that it had been kept cherished and safe in Hinata's treasure box.

"Maybe Neji'd be mad at me," Hinata said. "For showing it to you."

"Yeah, but you read it, right?" Naruto replied.

She nodded awkwardly and lowered her voice. "Just a little when I was sad. In secret."

Her saying that so quietly means he's definitely listening. He's such a fussy guy.

•

The next morning, Naruto got up early and stopped by the training ground before heading to the Hokage's office. He wanted to learn how to use the goggles as soon as possible to compensate for not using chakra.

The dewy grass reflected the pale morning sun, making the whole area glitter.

He closed his eyes and pulled the lever on the goggles.

Don't try to grasp all the chakra flowing through the keirakukei network. Gaze at the whole and predict the next chakra movement...

Reflecting on Neji's words, he slowly opened his eyes.

All the visual information in the area flooded into his retinas.

"Gaaaah!"

With a fierce cry, he tightened his grip on his fraying mind and braced himself. He could see all the things. He could feel a vein in his forehead throbbing. His optic nerves were at full throttle, on the edge of exploding.

Calm down. Choose what to see. You don't have to look at everything. First...a bird. I'll find a bird.

Naruto looked around. Dirt, stone, grass, dirt.

There.

There was a small bluish bird in the leaves of a tree. And not just one. Two, three... Five in total. He'd gotten that far when he reached his limit.

"Ngah! I can't!"

His eyes threatened to roll into the back of his head permanently, and Naruto ripped the goggles off. Surprised by his shout, the blue birds flew up into the air. One, two, three, four, five...

"There were eight of 'em!"

Naruto dropped to the ground. He had missed three whole birds. He still had a long, long way to go.

He looked up at the clouds slowly rolling through the sky and sighed. The vein in his forehead was still throbbing. He had no idea it would be this hard. Neji had never once let on that it was a struggle.

"That guy really was a genius..."

Narrow down the target, focus on that.

Close off sound and smell, concentrate on seeing only with the eyes.

The day before, Naruto had stayed up late reading the notes in the familiar hand that Neji had left behind. The thought that Neji could have taught him himself if he were alive made Naruto's eyes suddenly grow hot, and the tearstain he'd made on the cherished keepsake was a secret from Hinata.

The advice Neji had jotted down was a tremendous source of strength for Naruto. The efficiency of his training would improve from learning how to implement a deceptively simple mechanism of the tool.

"Woooohaky!" He leaped to his feet and slapped his cheeks. "Let's do this!"

After that, Naruto threw himself into his Byakugan training. He'd always had better-than-average reflexes and senses. As he drilled away day after day, he was able to endure the Byakugan for longer and longer, if only bit by bit.

And then, one afternoon...

Taking advantage of a break in his work, Naruto climbed to the top of Hokage Rock. He wanted to test out the Byakugan in a spot with a much richer view than the training ground.

He pulled the lever on the goggles and looked out over the old city. With fewer obstructions, the amount of information coming in was of a different magnitude from what he was used to at the training ground. On top of that, chakra-filled shinobi were wandering around all over the place, which was very distracting.

"Ngh..." He forced himself to focus his field of vision and spotted an unnatural chakra flow.

He turned his mind that way and found chakra leaking like a fog from the base of an old camphor tree on a narrow residential street.

"Hm? What's that?"

Does chakra usually come out of tree roots?

Naruto leaped down from Hokage Rock and went to check it out.

The camphor tree stood in a quiet area with few people passing by, even in the middle of the old city. The chakra wasn't being emitted by the tree roots themselves, but rather appeared to be leaking out from openings in the ground. Unless a shinobi had been buried alive in that spot, it was probably coming from a room underground.

There was a traditional townhouse in front of the camphor tree. The high windows were cracked, the gable was on an incline, and the structure looked quite abandoned.

"Helloooo?" Naruto opened the unlocked door and found dust piled up on the entryway floor. The old owner had apparently been some kind of merchant—an abacus lay on the step up into the house, and there was a bookcase next to the window.

"No stairs?"

He saw a large Japanese-style room, but he couldn't spot anything that looked like stairs in the bungalow.

Wait.

Naruto touched the hand that was not a prosthetic to the wall in the entryway.

Of course. The texture was the same as the liquid crystal wall in Tami's sweet shop.

When he examined the surface closely, he found a small black hole in amongst the woodgrain and knots. This was probably the keyhole. In which case, there had to be a key somewhere.

Prime suspects were the bookmark tucked into an old book and the long metal cooking chopsticks stabbed into the ashes in the brazier. The old-style pipe on the bookcase was also a possibility.

He hit the jackpot with his third choice, the pipe. There was a rattling sound inside the hole, and then the wall abruptly turned transparent. He pushed it lightly, and it opened toward the inside like a door.

The crystals throughout the panel were forced into arrays with electricity, resulting in the image of a detailed surface. It had been invented at the research institute, but because the technology hadn't yet been scaled up to mass production, it shouldn't have been out in the wild like this.

Which meant that whoever was here was connected with the institute?

On the other side of the wall was an old wooden staircase. The flames of evenly spaced lamps illuminated the steps in the gloom.

"This is way too dodgy." On guard, Naruto began down the stairs on quiet feet.

He found a sliding door at the bottom of the stairs, and when he opened it, he saw a large Japanese-style room with tatami mats on the floor. A kettle hanging from a pothook was whistling over a small sunken fireplace. There was a tea caddy on a low tray table, and tea leaves for one had been set out inside the overturned lid. Someone had clearly been in the middle of boiling water for tea.

"What is this place..."

The smoke from the fireplace was escaping to the outside through a vent, and what appeared to be a fire alarm was affixed to a fat joist on the ceiling. The modern fixture had at some point been installed in the old traditional space. He could sense someone hiding on the other side of the sliding doors further back in the room.

Naruto considered how to draw out the person from behind the door without alarming them when the door slid open.

"Intruder! Ready yourself!" A young woman in a coverall apron came flying out.

Kashunk!

He heard the sound of a scientific ninja tool, and a ball of flames roared to life to fill the small room. Naruto leaped up onto the joist to handily dodge it, and then dropped down behind the woman and plucked away the scientific ninja tool.

"Be careful," he told her. "You'll set the place on fire."

"Let go! You came to steal my research data, didn't you?!" With her wrist in Naruto's hand, the woman struggled and kicked like a mouse caught in a trap. "You dirty coward! Just let me go! You—! You!"

Belatedly, the fire alarm began to ring shrilly, and sprinklers in the ceiling began to spray water over the room.

"Well, I *did* come in without asking, so there's that." Feeling guilty, Naruto let go of her wrist, and the woman not only did not try to run away, she grabbed a pen from the pocket of her apron.

"You! Youuuuuuu!"

She came at him with it, swinging wildly. She had her eyes closed, so she didn't seem to catch on that Naruto was easily sidestepping her would-be blows.

"You came to steal my data! Isn't that right?!"

What is with *this woman?*

She attacked relentlessly for a full five minutes until she finally realized that it was the Seventh Hokage she was facing and regained a modicum of calm.

"I am so terribly sorry. I just misunderstood. My name is Ameno Chihare. I'm a scientist from the Land of Fire. My specialization is astrophysics." The woman bowed at the Hokage as she introduced herself.

The room had become thoroughly drenched from the kerfuffle. The water she'd boiled was completely cold now, after being showered in sprinkler water. Naruto and Chihare sat formally on their knees on the damp tatami mats and waited for the kettle to come to a boil over the fireplace once more.

"I scared you by just walking in here," Naruto said.

"No, my behavior was inexcusable," she responded. "I never imagined it would be the Seventh Hokage who came to take my research data."

"No, actually, you've got the wrong idea," he protested, exhausted, and looked up toward the stairs. "But why're you doing research or whatever in a place like this? Going to all the trouble of hiding this room with a liquid crystal wall. Those things are expensive, you know."

"I made it myself, so it didn't cost very much at all." Chihare took the boiling kettle off of the pothook and poured hot water into the teapot as she continued. "The liquid crystal wall is my design."

"Huh?" Naruto blinked rapidly in surprise. "So then you're a scientist at Kengakuin? What are you doing down here?"

"I wanted an environment where I could concentrate on my experiments alone," she said. "This house belongs to Director Furieh. He renovated the basement for research purposes, and I've been borrowing it."

It must have been some seriously important research if the basement had to be renovated.

Naruto looked around the room. "The truth is, I came here because I saw chakra leaking out from where this basement is. I was worried something dangerous might be going on. What's this research you're doing?"

"Chakra is visible to you?" Chihare asked.

When Naruto explained about the function of the goggles, she nodded in understanding.

"I see. The chakra you observed most likely leaked out from my lab further back."

"Which is why I asked what experiment—" Naruto was cut off.

"It would actually be quicker for you to take a look." She set the kettle down on the tatami mat, stood up, and pulled open a double door built into the other end of the Japanese-style room. "This is my lab."

Naruto's jaw dropped.

Shelves lined the forty-five-square-meter room from floor to ceiling and wall to wall. Petri dishes were crammed into every available space on every single shelf. There were maybe hundreds, even thousands of them. The sight of so many items the same size in the same place was quite impressive and somewhat disturbing.

"These petri dishes contain liquefied chakra," Chihare told him. "My mission is to create a pluripotent chakra applicator."

"Pluri..." Naruto stared at her blankly.

"It's an experiment to change chakra into other substances artificially."

She picked up one of the petri dishes and shook it gently as she continued.

"Don't you think chakra's quite mysterious? It can become anything at all. It can be wind, fire, earth, water, electricity. Depending on the person, it can be transformed into lava or rubber even. Recently, some ninja have changed the component elements included in dirt with Earth Style to make glass and gemstones. There is no other energy that can change into such diverse forms."

"Hmm. I guess, yeah." The phenomenon of transforming chakra was so innate to Naruto that he'd never thought too hard about it before. But now that she mentioned it, she was exactly right.

"It has the potential to transform into anything according to the user," she continued. "If we could control this nature of the chakra scientifically... For instance, what if we could turn chakra into a valuable natural resource or precious metals? Don't you think there would be plenty of societal good in that?"

Developing a new energy source?

Naruto finally understood the purpose of her experiment. And it was true that if they could make that happen, they would no longer have to destroy nature to extract resources. Such a development would drastically change the energy situation in every country. If they could substitute chakra for all kinds of energy, then the Land of Fire, with the leading shinobi village of the Five Great Nations, might jump to first place as a major energy provider.

That was if she could actually make it work.

"Artificially transforming chakra," he said. "How do you do that?"

"How do *you* do it?" Chihare asked in response, staring into Naruto's eyes. "How on earth do you change chakra into wind?"

"Err." Naruto looked anywhere but at her. Ever since his episodes had begun, not only had he not changed chakra into wind, he hadn't even kneaded chakra. But normally he opened the palm of his hand and...

Wait. How do *I do it?*

"I go *thud* and then *bam*, I guess," Naruto replied earnestly, and hearing it, Chihare let out a sigh.

"All you shinobi say the same incomprehensible thing. Well, I'm sure the perception is difficult to put into words. But at the very least, you must work with the idea, the intention of trying to give the chakra the form of wind. Just like when you move your arms and legs, your brain gives the command to knead chakra, the chakra receives that, and changes."

She was right. As long as Naruto didn't have the intention of changing chakra into wind, the chakra flowing through his body wouldn't transform.

"And a command from the brain—it's an electrical signal. Which means that, for instance, when you use the Rasengan, your brain is giving your chakra something close to an electrical signal. Perhaps we can artificially change chakra into the Rasengan. Making that a reality is the focus of my experiments."

Chihare showed Naruto the petri dish in her hand. At the bottom of the flat glass dish was a viscous, transparent liquid.

"This petri dish contains chakra I made into a liquid with special technology. By giving different types of stimuli to this chakra and observing its behavior, I'm examining the state change mechanism."

"Stimuli?"

"There are a number of them. Electrical current, temperature change, physical shocks. At any rate, my search is quite exhaustive."

Chihare opened a notebook set against the end of the shelf, a record of her experiments thus far. It was filled with the conditions and results of experiments in neat, delicate characters.

Oxygen treatment followed by heat stimulus: 42.5°C, no reaction.
Oxygen treatment followed by heat stimulus: 42.6°C, no reaction.
Oxygen treatment followed by heat stimulus: 42.7°C, no reaction.

Raising or lowering the temperature, injecting drugs with electricity applied—she changed the amount and time bit by bit, repeating the experiment under a variety of different conditions.

"Hey?" Naruto asked. "What's this 'jellyfish stimulus' here?"

"It's extract from a jellyfish," Chihare replied. "Research shows that it emits a stimulus similar to the electrical signal of the brain, so I tried introducing it to the chakra. But I didn't get any hits."

"Wow." Naruto sighed in genuine admiration.

Doing the same work over and over for an extended period required patience and perseverance. And with no guarantee that this effort would bear fruit, it must have been tough to keep pushing forward. No wonder she'd want so desperately to protect her data.

"There's one other thing I want you to see. I have it set outside though," Chihare said, and the two of them went up the stairs and out of the house, not using the front door with the camphor tree but, instead, the back door that faced the alley.

A vehicle with two tires was parked there, leaning against the shrubs.

"What's this?" he asked. "A cart? It's kind of an odd shape for that though."

"It's a system bike. You use it to go places. This is the seat." Chihare straddled the seat to show him. Her forward-leaning posture was like she was on horseback.

"You can go places on this?!" he cried. "That's super handy!"

Unlike the experiment for chakra pluripotency, Naruto immediately grasped this one.

The development of a vehicle for individual use had been a topic of discussion since the time of the Sixth Hokage. Development had progressed centered around the institute and Katasuke's research team, but fuel was a constant issue.

"This bike burns gas to move," Chihare explained. "The Land of Fire mainly imports gas from the Land of Wind and the Land of Kizahashi, right? But if we keep taking natural gas, it will run out at some point."

Given its serious dependence on trade, the Land of Kizahashi in particular was extracting gas without limit, but in the Land of Wind, the Kazekage had already begun to put limits on exports. His pretext was to keep prices from dropping too low, but he likely also wanted to prevent the gas from being depleted before an alternative energy source could be developed.

Chihare rapped lightly on the small tank attached to the bike.

"I'd like to revitalize personal transportation, but there's not enough fuel for everyone to go riding around. But my research might resolve that concern. If I can transform chakra and artificially produce Kizahashi gas for fuel, then we would no longer be dependent on the unstable supply from other countries."

"Amazing!" Naruto cried with childlike glee, his eyes shining. "If you can make that happen, then everyone'll get to ride one of these and go wherever they want whenever they want!"

"Yes, well. That's the idea."

When he stared directly at her, Chihare averted her eyes, looking anxious. "If you're thinking that way, I wish you'd help with my experiment. Would you, um, let me borrow the goggles that let you see chakra?"

"Huh? These?" Naruto touched the frame of the goggles.

Chihare pulled a glass stick out of her pocket. "I use this 'scouter' measurement device to see if the chakra in the petri dishes has transformed. I bring the tip of the scouter close to the liquefied chakra and check if the numbers are different from the previous day. But it's quite time-intensive. I have to go around and measure each and every one of them. If I could confirm visually using those goggles, I would finish faster."

"Ohh. Sure, I can lend them to you." He himself had borrowed them from Orochimaru, but he quickly decided that Orochimaru wouldn't particularly care if he passed them on. "But I don't think you'll be able to use them if you just throw them on without any training. I still haven't quite gotten the hang of them, and I'm a shinobi."

"What?!"

Despair raced across Chihare's face upon hearing that even the Hokage couldn't master them. "Then they'll be absolutely impossible for *me* to use. Oh! I know. You could just come here every day and check the flow of chakra for me!"

"That's more than 'just' a request, you know," he protested weakly. "I have stuff to do too."

"Are you busy?" she asked. "But if you used the Teleportation Jutsu, you could be here instantly."

"Oh. I can't use chakra right now." Even though he'd been keeping it a secret from everyone in the village, for some reason, the words came naturally from his mouth. Maybe the ease of talking to someone he didn't know made him say it.

"What?!" Chihare was at a loss for words and looked at Naruto pityingly. "What is the point for you when you can't use chakra?"

She was powerfully direct, stabbing straight into his heart.

"The biggest reason that Uzumaki Naruto became the Seventh Hokage was because of how highly valued his achievements in the Great Ninja War were, right? Meaning, basically, that the people were seeking battle power from you, and now you can't use chakra, which seems bad. Will you continue as Hokage?"

I'm not giving up the Hokage seat to anyone!

The old Naruto would almost certainly have yelled something like that. But right now, as Hokage, he bore different burdens than he did in the past. Could he continue as Hokage when he could no longer fight—this was the thought that had been stuck in his head all this time.

"My situation's one thing." Naruto awkwardly changed the subject. "But if I can help with your experiments, I'll do it. Not so much Hokage work at this time of year anyway."

"Thank you so much!" she cried. "It's settled then."

They marched down the stairs and returned to the lab to

get started right away and check the petri dishes. There were an incredible eight hundred of them on the shelves against one wall.

Naruto climbed the stepladder and pulled the lever on the goggles.

"Hmm."

He moved his eyes over the chakra in the dishes one by one, but all of it was sitting quietly in the bottoms of the glass dishes. He couldn't see any real changes.

"None of them are really moving and shaking here."

"Well, we won't see results that quickly," Chihare said. "I've been doing this for over six months now, but I still haven't found any chakra that's changed."

Six months—apparently, Byakugan training and scientific experiments were the same in that they both required repeated trial and error. But Naruto was nothing if not entirely up for a fight of perseverance and determination.

This actually only made him more determined as he looked at all the petri dishes lined up on the shelves.

Chihare's experiment had the potential to significantly change the world. If they could change the nature of chakra at will, allowing non-ninja to use it too, he was sure their world would become more convenient and a lot more fun. For instance—

"So, like, what if you completed this plooripotent machine?" Naruto said, the stepladder between his legs as he stepped with it to one side, holding onto the shelf as he did. "Copying Kizahashi gas is fine and all, but we could use it for other things too, right? Like—"

"You're saying you'd like to use it in the field of medical treatment. I understand that," Chihare cut him off and continued. "If chakra could be Kizahashi gas, then it might also become skin or nails or organs like the heart. If we can understand how to transform chakra into human cells, we'll be able to repair tissue lost in accidents or through illness. We should be able to dramatically extend healthy life expectancy."

"Right! I don't get all that difficult stuff," he replied. "But when I heard you talking about chakra, my first thought was maybe we could fix Sasuke's arm or Master Guy's leg."

"Sasuke? Do you mean—" Chihare started to ask if he was referring to Uchiha Sasuke.

Krrrrrnnk!

Suddenly, the ceiling split open, and wooden boards dropped down. Shelves broke, and petri dishes slid to the floor and shattered.

"What the—?!" Naruto grabbed Chihare's arm and pulled her in front of him to protect her from the chunks of ceiling raining down on them.

A spherical multicopter with four propellers flew in through the opening in the ceiling, motor humming quietly—a drone. The machine used lift generated by the four propellers to fly. Naruto had read reports about drone research at the institute and by Katasuke, but this was the first time he'd actually seen one.

So they did it then? Naruto forgot for a moment the situation they were in and stared at it.

Perceiving Naruto's gaze as a threat, the drone approached with a whine.

Should I shoot it down before it attacks? But I don't know if it's hostile or not. What if it just made a mistake and flew in here during a test? Someone would be mad at me if I smashed it...

While he wrestled with what to do, the numeral five popped up on the central sphere of the drone.

Four, three, two. The numbers dropped before his eyes.
A bomb!

"Run!"

"Huh?"

Naruto flew out of the lab with Chihare in his arms. He raced up the flight of stairs, and about halfway up...

Boom!

"Yikes!"

Blowback from the explosion pushed up from the bottom of the stairs. Still clutching Chihare, he forced his way up the crumbling stairs and made it out onto the ground floor. He kicked down the door, and as they ran out onto the street, he heard the hum of a drone approaching.

"What was that?! An explosion?! Was that a *drone*? A real one?!" Chihare yelped, panicking, and Naruto pushed her behind him without a word.

New drones appeared one after the other. Seven of them, arranged in a fan formation with the central drone in the lead. Naruto could tell someone was clearly controlling them, but where? And more importantly, who? The incident with Aze Yanaru crossed his mind, but he had no proof that the same person was pulling the strings here.

What he did know was that if these drones all exploded together, it wouldn't just be the empty house that went up in flames. He needed to get them away from the crowded city, but in his current chakra-less state, where could he go?

Twenty-eight propellers played their whirring song, interrupting Naruto's thoughts. He divided his attention among the machines lined up neatly before them, and then he heard a new sound cut through the air—an engine roaring to life.

"Please get on! You drive!" Chihare shouted, straddling the seat of a bike and pulling on the engine lever.

Taking advantage of the moment Naruto was distracted, the seven drones began to move as one. Naruto dodged the machines dive-bombing his face, grabbing a plastic bucket from where it lay on the road and throwing it over the closest drone.

And for good measure, he kicked the lid of the bucket up at the remaining drones. This counterattack slowed the machines briefly, but they were soon back in formation.

Thoom! Thoom!

The imprisoned drone pulverized its plastic bucket cage in no time with its propellers and flew out to freedom.

"Gah! Come *on!*"

Naruto threw the remaining buckets at them with an air of desperation, and then turned his back boldly to run full speed toward the bike. He leaped onto it, grabbed the handlebars, and straddled the seat.

"Grab the lever, and press down on the right foot pedal!" Chihare said.

"Which one's the lever?!" he yelled.

"This one!" She reached out from behind and slapped the lever below the right handgrip.

Vrrrm!

The engine roared, the bike leaped up, and in the recoil, Naruto's foot slammed down onto the pedal. He felt a sudden force pushing on the rear of the machine.

"Wha?!" he yelped, and the bike shot forward like a rocket.

The scenery streamed past, and the wind pushed against his face, making it hard to keep his eyes open. When he took a hand off the grips to lower his goggles, the bike swerved dramatically, and the righthand mirror hit the concrete block wall on one side of the road and catapulted up into the air.

"Whoa!"

"Could you please keep your balance here?" Chihare complained, but she herself knew only too well that it was an absurd request. He was already driving impossibly well given that this was his first time even being on the unwieldy machine.

His reflexes were good, and now that he'd experienced losing his balance once, Naruto took one hand off the grip again, but this time, the bike kept moving in a straight line. He lowered his goggles, pulled the lever, and put his hand back on the grip. He checked out the view behind them with his Byakugan. There were no drones around.

"Hey, Chihare!" he shouted. "How do you stop this thing?"

"You can't stop it," she replied curtly.

"What?!"

"I told you it's a prototype, didn't I?! Incidentally, you also can't adjust the speed!"

The ends of the grips brushed up against the hedges in front of houses. The road was fairly narrow, and it just barely accommodated the bike.

The machine would stop once it ran out of fuel. But Naruto didn't want to think about what would happen first—the gas tank emptying out, or the bike crashing through one of the houses on either side of the road.

Well, the road *was* narrow, but he could probably make it as long as he kept driving straight like this. Wait. Where were they, anyway?

He glanced around and caught sight of blackish blobs flying at the edge of his field of vision through the goggles. "They came after us!"

The seven drones were closing in on them impossibly fast.

A muzzle shaped like a straw stretched out from the spherical body of the drone in the lead.

Hm?

Naruto turned his attention to it and saw the tip flash red.

The photon gun confiscated from Aze Yanaru emits an excimer laser, and the structure is such that the muzzle of the gun flashes red before it fires...

This line from the report on the assassination attempt in the Land of Kizahashi popped up in his mind.

Yikes!

Vvvn!

A bright red beam of light shot out with a low hum, the sound of photons knocking molecules aside.

Naruto didn't know anything about how to operate this bike, but he reflexively tilted the vehicle body. Their path forward shifted to one side, and the laser beam passed just above his ear and shot into the hedge of a nearby house.

Bompf!

The reed screen in front of the hedges swelled up and exploded at the sudden and dramatic increase in temperature.

"Impossible..." They would die if they took a hit from that. Chihare grabbed tightly onto Naruto's shoulders. "Please get us out of here! This road is too narrow! Go out onto the main street!"

"Can't. Too many people on that road. We have to get out of the village—" Before he could finish his sentence, a laser beam shot out from the left this time. It hit the block wall squarely, and a cat startled by the explosion shot out across the road.

"Cat!" Chihare cried.

"I know!" Naruto shouted.

The block wall crumbled, the rubble piling up and spilling out into the middle of the street. When the front wheel of the bike hit the block wall, Naruto threw his arms out and shifted his center of gravity backward.

The front tire floated up. The bike rose up into the air, like it had hit a spring, and easily flew over the cat's head before hitting the ground again with a *thud*.

"Aaah!"

The bike stopped for a moment, pitching forward, before restarting its relentless charge forward.

Chihare bit her tongue she screamed so hard, and now she shouted into Naruto's ear with tears in her eyes. "Lord Seventh! If we're trying to leave the village, the A-un gate is the other way!"

"Can't." Naruto shook his head. "To go out the gate, we have to go down the main road. Too much of a risk of damage to the village."

"Well then how are we going to get out?"

A way to get outside without going through the gate—train or airship.

"I got it," he said in a low voice and clenched the grips.

The train station was on the other side of the main street, a long stucco building with three large doors. The doors had been a gift from the Kazekage to celebrate the opening of the railway, and tourists flocked to them to admire the beauty of their construction, with mother-of-pearl inlay craftsmanship and detailed gold lacquer decoration.

"Outta the waaaaay!"

The Seventh Hokage sent the bike charging into one of those beautiful, big doors. The door, cruelly sent flying hinges and all, collided with two of the seven drones and unexpectedly cut the number of their pursuers.

The five remaining drones got back into formation and zoomed forward.

Vvvn vvvn vvvvvvvnnnnnnnnn!

The bike engine roaring, they raced along the wooden floor inside the station building. The stunned passengers who happened to be in the building fled in a panic and, no doubt, never even imagined that the maniacal rider of this rampaging machine was the Seventh Hokage. Tires squealing, the bike screeched down the stairs while Naruto broke off the remaining left mirror and threw it at the emergency alarm when they came out onto the platform.

Eeeeeeeeeeeeeeee!

The mirror hit the button smack in the middle, and a shrill alarm filled the air. The bike slipped through the pandemonium of the platform, shrieks and curses coming from all corners, and out onto the line itself to race alongside the train that had come to an emergency stop.

"Chihare! Don't bite your tongue!" Naruto cautioned, unaware that she had already bitten it once. Unlike the paved streets of the old city, the railway line was a bumpy road of railroad ties at regular intervals. Each time they went over a tie, the bike slid from side to side, but Naruto quickly righted them by shifting his center of gravity.

"We're getting out of the village. I'll figure out what to do about them once there's no one around!"

As he rode, Naruto kept an eye on the pursuers behind them. Five drones left. Only two had come at them with the laser beams. The drones had had any number of chances, but none of them had tried to suicide bomb Naruto and Chihare. So then was it just that one drone at the start equipped with a bomb?

Thump!

His heart pounded heavily, and a sudden pain radiated through his chest. One hand nearly slipped off the grip, and he hurried to tighten his fingers around it again. But the hand trembled and shook.

"Ngh... Not. Now..."

The crushing pain in his chest pulsed and throbbed more intensely with each passing second. He started to wheeze and gasp for breath. It was like his trachea was refusing to let oxygen pass.

Chihare noticed something was wrong with him. "What's the matter?!"

"Noth...ing!" Naruto bluffed hard and yanked his face up. The wind pushing up against them sent the cold sweat beading on his forehead scattering behind them. He put an elbow on the tank and rubbed his eyes, his vision hazy and pale, as he desperately panted for air.

"Hey, are you having trouble? Is this bad?!" Chihare panicked.

"I can't take over the driving, you know?!"

Behind her, the drones were getting closer.

"Come on already!" Naruto leaned to the side to dodge a laser beam and slammed his aching chest against the tank. He could taste blood from where he'd bitten his lip.

The railroad track led out onto a steel bridge. Below the bridge was a valley with a brook running through it.

Abruptly, two of the drones on their tail cut out to the side.

Huh? They give up?

Naruto watched the drones with the Byakugan as they dove under the bridge and shot laser beams at the arched piers supporting it.

The steel was burning bright red in an instant, and sparks began to fly.

"For real?" He gaped at the sight.

Boom!

An explosion knocked the pier away from the base.

"They went and smashed the pillar!" he yelled indignantly.

The tracks rose up like inchworms, the guardrails shattered, and the railroad ties bounced up into the air. Having lost its road, the front wheel of the bike bounced up almost perfectly perpendicular.

"Do you know how much it cost to build this bridge?!" he shouted.

"Is now really the time to worry about that?!" Chihare yelled back.

Without its pier, the bridge started to crumble from below. Naruto selected a rail that was still more or less retaining its shape and desperately kept riding, but he soon reached its limit. Rail twisted apart and thrust up to knock the rear wheel of the bike away, and the force of it pushed Naruto and Chihare into empty air.

"Dammit..."

Of all the times not to be able to use chakra!

Naruto twisted his torso, wrapped an arm around Chihare's waist, and assumed a passive falling posture with himself on the bottom. They were surrounded by twisted railway, thick pylons, and all manner of debris that could kill them instantly if they got trapped under it, but thanks to the Byakugan, he was pretty sure he could swim them through it and make it safely to the ground.

And then a drone appeared before him, gun muzzle out.

Naruto didn't even have time to groan before the extended barrel locked onto his eyes. The tip blinked with red light.

"...!"

To protect Chihare, he switched positions with her just as the branch of a tree shot out and stabbed the drone from directly below.

The red light vanished, and the four propellers slowed to a stop.

The extended branch kept moving to wrap around Naruto and Chihare and catch them in midair.

This. This was Wood Style ninjutsu.

"No way..."

There was currently only one person in the village of Konohagakure who had this kind of command over Wood Style.

Naruto looked up with a gasp and saw that an enormous tree had grown up from the valley to support the crumbling steel bridge. Swirling vines curled tightly around it and stabilized the structure.

Moving like a creature with its own will, the tree branch lowered Naruto and Chihare to the ground. As it slackened and twisted away from them, Chihare slumped down to the ground with a wretched, "Haah."

"I see you're just barely alive as always, Naruto," came a flat voice, together with the crunch of gravel.

Naruto patted his chest, the painful attack now past, and exhaled briefly before looking back.

The star of the Anbu was standing tall, hands still woven in a sign. Face guard hiding the outline of his face. And Wood Style ninjutsu inherited from the genes of the First Hokage.

"Commander...Yamato..."

Yamato, the man who had once led Naruto in place of Kakashi, saw that Naruto was unharmed and smiled in relief.

Chapter 3

"You were attacked by drones?!"

For once, Shikamaru was visibly upset. Drones using excimer lasers were definitely not the sort of thing the average person could whip up. This kind of development didn't happen without a scientist on the level of Katasuke or the involvement of an international research agency.

"Just to check, you didn't sense any chakra?"

"None at all." Naruto shook his head. "I checked with the Byakugan too, so there's no mistake."

"Hmm." Shikamaru put a hand to his chin. "How about we ask Professor Katasuke if he's heard any rumors about the development of battle drones? We could also try asking Furieh some leading questions."

"Leading questions?" Naruto arched an eyebrow. "Like what?"

Shikamaru glanced up at the ceiling. The donut-shaped device set in the center was made to look like a fire alarm, but it actually detected listening devices. The light on the device was not flashing, confirming the room was clean, so he lowered his voice and said, "The assassination attempt in the Land of Kizahashi. The research institute might have been behind it."

"What?!"

"The Anbu got ahold of info that shows contact between Furieh and the guy who did it, Aze Yanaru."

Naruto scowled. "Is there any solid evidence that he's behind it?"

"If there was, I'd have had shinobi on him ages ago," Shikamaru replied. "But there isn't any, so we're stuck."

Konoha had asked the institute to help decipher the literature concerning the Land of Redaku. Of course, they hadn't mentioned Naruto's illness, but that didn't change how risky the contact for assistance was.

Shikamaru frowned and crossed his arms. "I don't want to give more info to someone we don't know if we can trust, but... The institute's the highest authority when it comes to deciphering ancient texts. To be honest, we're not getting anywhere with analysis of the stuff on Redaku. We don't have much of a choice but to rely on them."

He'd gotten an email from the team at the institute that morning with their analysis of the text Kakashi had sent. It included specific notes on the method used to cure the Sage of Six Paths' illness.

Wasting away from a curious illness, the Sage of Six Paths had cause to attend the Land of Redaku and thus did meet the astronomer Tatar on his path.

Ministered to by this Tatar, his illness nonetheless troubled him yet.

One evening, Tatar espied a meteor approaching the land. The Sage of Six Paths caught this fallen meteorite in hand and split it in twain in a singular motion.

A bright light spilled forth from the halved meteorite to bathe the

Sage of Six Paths. Instantly, the Sage was freed of his illness of
many years.

   The meteor which fell from the heavens presented him with
blessed strength, allowing his chakra to expand without limit. Tatar
named the substance in the meteor that was the source of his power
"ultra particles."

   To stop those who would struggle for this grand power he held,
he hid half of these ultra particles in "the sky that fell to the earth,"
and the other half in "the star that never strays."

   The ultra particles sleep in this world well-protected by a path
lined with stars.

   Should others be consumed with the illness of the Sage of Six
Paths, they are destined to desire the power of the ultra particles. And
thus this distant power will be made to come to this distant land.

   Any who would seek out this state must tarry in the Land of
Redaku reveling with the Map of the Heavens.

   Basically, if they could get ahold of these "ultra particles"
or whatever they were that the Sage of Six Paths hid in "the
sky that fell to the earth" and "the star that never strays," they
could cure Naruto's illness. Hawks had already been sent to
Kakashi and Sakura to let them know the details of this text.
If their investigations went well, they would send further clues.
If those clues were written in the ancient tongue of Redaku,
then Shikamaru would ask the institute to decipher them again,
in full awareness of the danger that posed.

   Cautious Shikamaru was choosing to take such risks
because of Naruto. Because of him, everyone was forced to cross
dangerous bridges. Naruto bit his lip.

   Shikamaru smiled suddenly in exasperation. "Don't get
that tiresome look on your face. It's not like you."

   "I don't have a look on my face." Naruto averted his eyes but
unconsciously pursed his lips.

Of course he was concerned about this illness, but more than that, he was frustrated that he couldn't do anything about it himself. The Naruto of the old days wouldn't have hesitated to head for the Land of Redaku himself and look for a cure. But the Naruto of now couldn't do that.

The Seventh Hokage couldn't be away from the village for long periods, especially for his own needs. The number of things he had the authority to do had grown since he became Hokage, but at the same time, the number of things he couldn't do had also increased. It was a weighty position.

"Don't overthink this," Shikamaru told him. "You just do your Hokage thing like always. That's what's most important for this village."

"Yeah. I know that." Naruto pulled over a stack of papers on the edge of his desk and set his chin on it. He felt a prickling pain in his chest and braced himself for another episode, but it wasn't that. This time the prickling was his frustration coupled with a dull heaviness that tugged at his core.

"Hey, Shikamaru?" he said.

"Hm?" His friend looked at him.

"What if."

What if I never have chakra again... How could I protect the village?

He swallowed the words that started to come out and looked for something else to follow that "what if" with.

"What if... Is it possible the drones weren't attacking me, but that researcher Chihare who was with me?"

Shikamaru thought for a second. "If Kengakuin really is behind this, then I guess it's possible. She's with them, right?"

"Not so much with them. She's a scientist there," Naruto said. "For some reason, she was doing her research alone in the basement of a house instead of at the institute. Weird, huh?"

"But the house was destroyed by the drones," Shikamaru commented. "Where's she working now?"

Naruto averted his eyes. "I talked to this scientist I know, and he offered her a lab."

"You know a scientist?"

When Naruto told him the name of this scientist, Shikamaru's expression grew stern.

Afternoon.

Naruto visited Chihare's new lab to help with her experiment as promised.

It was a desolate facility built in a cave in the valley with the steel bridge across it. The place itself had done nothing wrong, but the further he went into the cave, the more he felt the oppressive air.

The researchers in this place were all a bunch of bad characters, but their skills were sharp—Suigetsu, Karin, and Orochimaru. Chihare was borrowing one of Orochimaru's labs.

Of course, Konoha was definitely not allowing this trio to run as they pleased. Yamato was always monitoring the situation, keeping a close eye on their movements.

"You were a real lifesaver showing up yesterday, Commander Yamato," Naruto said, and his words echoed slightly against the rock of the cave. He crouched down and whispered to Yamato behind the rock wall near the entrance. "Sorry for all this, for leaving you to watch over Orochimaru."

"That's just how it has to be. There's no one who can take over for me after all."

Yamato had basically carried the burden of observing Orochimaru's group since the days of the last Hokage. The man himself almost certainly didn't view his mission in terms of advantage and disadvantage, but it was clear that the burden was concentrated on him alone. Kakashi had looked into improving the situation numerous times, as had Naruto and Shikamaru, but they hadn't really been able to find anything better than Yamato. As Yamato himself said, there was no one else who could take his place.

Naruto sensed someone coming in from outside and pressed himself to the ceiling. Yamato stayed where he was hidden behind the protruding rock.

"Hello, Yamato!" Mitsuki appeared on unusually quiet feet for a genin. He had just finished a mission with the Konohamaru team and stopped in for a visit.

"Mitsuki." Yamato looked back, still on his knees. "You're early. How was the mission?"

"Finding a lost cat and cleaning culverts," the boy replied. "Boruto fell in the river, but other than that, we finished without any issues."

"Those are both D-rank missions?" Yamato raised his eyebrows. "I would have thought you'd find missions like that a bit lacking."

"To be honest, I do a little. Since we finished early, Boruto, Shikadai, and Inojin stopped by the burger place in front of the station."

Naruto looked down on the pair smiling at each other with a curious feeling. This gentle conversation was like something between an elementary school kid and an older neighbor man.

Mitsuki at last bowed politely and went into the laboratory. Naruto waited for the sound of his footsteps to fade and then dropped down from the ceiling.

"Commander Yamato, you're kind of right at home, huh?"

"Well, when I'm here twenty-four seven, you know?" Yamato smiled like even he was exasperated with himself, and then his face tightened again. "But you can't trust a one of them. Orochimaru might seem quiet these days, but you never know what he's thinking deep down. And those guys in the Taka, they're pretty idiosyncratic. You can't let your guard down."

Now Karin came from within to see Yamato.

While Naruto watched from the rocky shadow of the ceiling to which he hurriedly returned, Karin took a plate with a strawberry daifuku on it and a cup of green tea off the tray she carried and set them down on top of a rock.

"Yamato, have a snack," she said. "Mitsuki got enough daifuku for you too."

"I told him, I'm good," Yamato protested. "I'm on duty here."

"Oh, quit that. Mitsuki went out of his way to get one for you, so just be quiet and eat it. Bring the plate back when you're done!" Grumbling, Karin went back to the lab.

Yamato sighed and looked at the strawberry daifuku and its light dusting of flour with a troubled expression.

"Commander Yamato," Naruto said. "Are you sure you're not letting your guard down?"

"I told you, I'm not."

Leaving Yamato to continue his observation mission, Naruto went to visit the lab for real.

He couldn't exactly visit as a proper guest, ringing the doorbell with a little gift for his host in hand. He simply walked in and wandered around until he ran into Suigetsu.

"Aah! Seventh Hokage! I'd heard you were coming, but you really are here, hm? In a place like this," Suigetsu said, his voice light. The corners of his mouth were dusted with white powder. Probably from the strawberry daifuku.

"Where's Chihare?" Naruto asked.

"This way, come on." Suigetsu started to walk on ahead of him but then slackened his pace and waited until he was beside Naruto before starting out again. Orochimaru was apparently in another lab that day. "The experiment she's doing...developing an applicator for pluripotent chakra? Was that it? It's a lot of work, hm? There are so many different stimuli to try on the chakra; it takes an enormous amount of time. A lot to take on all on her own."

"If you've got the time to sit around eating strawberry daifuku, then give her a hand," Naruto replied.

"How did you know I was eating strawberry daifuku?" Suigetsu stared at him in surprise. "And anyway, me and Karin both asked if we could help. But she absolutely refused to let us."

Refused?

"Why would she...?" Naruto said.

Suigetsu cocked his head to one side. "No idea," he said, not sounding like he cared either way. "There are a lot of researchers who want to keep the results all to themselves."

The facility was enormous, with countless rooms. He could hear a sound like liquid boiling violently; the place was somehow not quiet. Whenever Naruto turned his eyes toward a door, Suigetsu gleefully asked if he'd like to see inside, grinning toothily, so each time, Naruto shook his head.

Once they had turned a number of corners and moved quite far inside the lab, Suigetsu stopped.

"This is it." He pointed at a heavy iron door built into the end of the hallway. "And I'll tell you one thing right now. Orochimaru almost never lends anyone a part of his own lab. You can't possibly think he's just being nice, right?"

"I know." Naruto nodded and pushed on the door. "That's just how valuable her work is, I guess."

Chihare was sitting on the linoleum floor and working at the computer on the low table that had been brought in for her. There were also a desk and chair against the wall, but she couldn't really focus unless she was working in the setup she was used to using.

While she was hunched over and reexamining her test results, she heard the sound of the door opening.

"Chihare! I'm here!"

It was Naruto.

She stood up slowly, slipped between the steel shelves that filled the lab space, and poked her head out. "Thanks for coming."

"Sure." He smiled at her and then frowned. "Uh, you have huge bags under your eyes."

"I haven't slept," she told him. "The amenities are good here, so I'm making nice progress with my tests."

Although the hallways and the entrance of Orochimaru's lab were decorated with the rustic beauty of bare rock face, one step inside of any room revealed the most modern of facilities. The walls and ceiling were stainless steel that shone silver, the air conditioning could be adjusted in units of 0.1 percent of a degree, and there was even a clean room in the back.

Once she'd been given the blessing of these amenities, Chihare's research had become visibly more efficient. Working here was better in every way than in a renovated Japanese-style room in the basement of a house. To start with, the space was large, so the number of shelves she could set up and the number of petri dishes she could put on them had tripled. The steel shelves were crowded together and so completely filled with glass petri dishes, it was like they shunned extra space.

Cameras were positioned openly near the ceiling. Everything about the experiment was being recorded, it seemed. Which meant that her results, if any, would be shared whether she liked it or not, but she had expected that much at least when she'd agreed to work in Orochimaru's lab.

"Okay, let's get right to it!" Naruto exclaimed and turned his goggles on.

Even though the number of petri dishes had clearly increased, he didn't utter a word of complaint as he promptly got on with the work of checking the chakra in them. There was little space between the shelves, making it a fairly tight fit for someone Naruto's size.

"So, Suigetsu was telling me." He started talking to Chihare while he put a foot on the edge of a lower shelf and grabbed onto the ceiling with both hands to peer at the dishes on the very top shelf. "You told them you don't need their help?"

"Yes." She nodded. "I've done it all by myself up to now."

"But wouldn't you finish faster if you got them to help you?"

"It's fine. It's very stressful when there's another person here."

"Is that it?" Naruto said as if understanding. He fell silent, but soon enough, he turned his face toward her with a gasp. "But you did ask *me* to come, right?"

Well, yes, she did. It was painful for her to have other people around, so she'd been doing her research in that basement by herself. But for some reason, she'd naturally reached out to Naruto. When she thought about it, it was curious.

I wonder why...

While Chihare blinked rapidly in confusion, Naruto went ahead and found his own reason. "Oh! I guess because the goggles are handy." And got back to work.

Yes, right. That was it. The goggles. She wanted to borrow the power of the goggles. That was why she'd reached out to him. Otherwise, she would never deliberately choose to be in the same space as another person.

"I've never really been comfortable with other people around," she muttered, and Naruto turned a confused face toward her.

"You like being alone better?" he asked. "I like being with the whole gang myself."

"But then you have to walk on eggshells, trying to get along," she said. "Isn't it easier when you're alone?"

"Well, I guess some people are like that," he mused. "But, you know, there's a lot of fun you can have when someone else is around."

"Such as?" Chihare asked in return.

"Right." Naruto looked out into space. "The one that still cracks me up is back when Master Kakashi had just become Hokage." He abruptly burst out laughing.

A bit excessive, laughing at a memory. He grinned so happily that Chihare nearly rolled her eyes.

"So we were told to go on this mission to take down this group of thieves," he continued. "And Sasuke just happened to be in the village, so he came along too. He's not a shinobi, strictly speaking, so he wasn't officially helping."

Uchiha Sasuke and Hatake Kakashi. He dropped these formidable names so casually, and Chihare was secretly impressed. He was strangely affable by nature, but this person really was the Seventh Hokage.

"The boss's name was Kinetsu, but Sasuke, he messed it up for some reason and kept calling the boss Kitsune. So through the whole strategy meeting, he's calling this guy Kitsune. And everyone noticed that he had the name wrong, but Sasuke had this real tough-guy air about him, so no one could tell him, and then it just got extra ridiculous."

"Did you keep yourself from laughing?" she asked.

"It was more like we didn't know if we should laugh or not," he replied. "The team split into two after that. I was with Kiba and Sakura. And Shino, I think. As soon as Sasuke was gone, Sakura whispers, 'He had the wrong name, right?' And then we all exploded, like 'Right?!' 'He totally had it wrong, right?!' And we laughed until we nearly died even though we were in the middle of a mission."

Naruto was unable to hold back his laughter anymore, and chuckles slipped out of him.

"This was honestly ages ago, and maybe none of them remember it now. But I do. And I still think it's hilarious."

"You do," she said flatly.

The floodgates having opened, Naruto proceeded to tell her all kinds of stories about his friends. How Choji sobbing his heart out at Sai and Ino's wedding was one thing, but even Shikamaru had cried a little. How they got a little too involved in playing the Game of Life and the new year arrived before they even realized it. How he and his friends had come together and racked their brains to come up with a plan to get Master Kakashi's mask off and see his bare face. How one time, Sai had poured his whole heart into the Cartoon Beast Mimicry drawing that was so scary they were all stunned. How before Naruto's marriage, Master Iruka and Sakura had given him intensive training in cooking, something he was not great at.

"I practiced a couple dishes over and over until I could make them super good, but that's it. Hinata was surprised at how good my cooking was. But the truth is, there were plenty of dishes buried in the dark before I showed her. Soggy chahan rice, curry with potato mush instead of chunks."

Naruto appeared to enjoy himself no matter who he was talking about. All of his stories were nothing more than little episodes that didn't matter one way or the other. Chihare found it strange that he could chat so happily about these other people. This person clearly liked his friends beyond reason.

He kept moving his eyes like a good worker as he chatted with her about this and that, and when he had checked the last petri dish, he dropped to the floor and announced dramatically, "It's no good. No change in any of them!"

"Is that right?" Chihare said simply.

"'Is that right'?" he parroted. "Come on, be a little more disappointed."

"It's normal that there isn't a result," Chihare said, her voice cool, and looked down at his blue eyes. "All your memories of your friends that you've been telling me about... To me, they all felt rather unnecessary."

She wondered if her honesty would make things awkward, but Naruto laughed as he slowly got to his feet. "I think so too. It's weird. They're all such teensy things, but I love those little details the most. Like when we're tired after work, or nothing's going so great and you're getting annoyed... When I remember stuff like that, it kind of cheers me up. Even though it's stupid."

"..."

Naruto's smile was innocent and carefree, and just looking at it was like a light turning on in her own heart. She was relieved, but she also felt guilty. The more Naruto told his happy stories, the greater guilt she felt toward herself for not being able to have those same emotions.

I'll never be loved by people like that.

"The fact that you care about the people around you came through very clearly," she told him.

Almost annoyingly so.

"But I'm not like you. I don't need connections with people." Feeling like she was making excuses for herself, Chihare continued quickly. "I don't feel lonely, and I've always mostly been alone. Although maybe someone like you who grew up loved by the people around you can't understand that."

Naruto started to say something, but eventually closed his slightly open mouth without uttering a single word.

•

It had been just over two weeks since Chihare moved to Orochimaru's lab.

Naruto spent his days moving back and forth and back again between the lab and his office and his house. The experiment continued to come up empty, and although the busy period for his Hokage duties had supposedly passed, since he couldn't use his shadow doppelgangers, his schedule was as full as ever. For whatever reason, his pain attacks were decreasing in frequency. Until very recently, he would curl into a ball several times a day, grit his teeth, and endure whatever was happening somewhere in his body. But in the last few days not a single one had occurred.

If the cause of his illness was poor functioning of the chakra channels, as Sakura had guessed, then maybe by some chance that had gotten better, and he was moving in a positive direction. Naruto was seriously starting to take this optimistic outlook when a hawk arrived at the Hokage's office from the astronomical observatory.

"She says the longer periods between attacks is actually not great." Shikamaru read the letter from Sakura and gave the news to Naruto straight up. "Your chakra's not recovering. The fact that only the attacks are gone in this state..."

"It's bad?" Naruto asked weakly.

"Well, we don't know. Anyway, they sent a huge clue for us." Shikamaru placed a book with a navy blue cover on the desk. It was large, the size of a picture book, and the hawk entrusted with carrying it had broken the spine. The cover had "Map of the Heavens" on it in gold leaf.

"I'll skip the details, but they found this *Map of the Heavens* at the observatory, along with the half of the ultra particles hidden in 'the sky that fell to the earth.' That's this." He then plonked a bamboo vessel plastered with protective wards on top of the desk. "It's sealing some seriously powerful chakra. Don't touch it."

"Do we know the signs to release it?" Naruto asked.

"Apparently, they're in here." Shikamaru tapped the book next to the bamboo vessel. The rule book for a card game called Star Lines. "Unfortunately, the ink in a key part is blurred and we can't read it. I'll send it to the institute and get them working on it."

"To the institute." Naruto frowned.

They kept passing critical information on to Kengakuin. On the surface, the institute appeared to be working with Naruto's office, but he had no idea what Director Furieh was actually planning.

Pretending that he didn't see Naruto's face cloud over, Shikamaru set a folded piece of straw paper next to the bamboo vessel. "Also. This was wedged into *Map of the Heavens*."

Naruto peered at the straw paper.

X Month X Day The stars increased.

The short bit of text was scribbled in cursive. Below the sentence was a whirlpool mark swirling to the left. A small triangle was attached to the bottom left of the whirlpool like a door stopper.

"This is...the mark of Konoha?" Naruto looked up at Shikamaru.

"Looks like it, huh?"

"What's this mean? They found this book in the Land of Redaku, right? Why would the mark of our village be in it?"

Peppered with questions, Shikamaru shrugged. "No idea. Might be the same symbol just happened to pop up somewhere else. We can't say anything for sure yet. At any rate, we have the ultra particles, so Sasuke and Sakura should be making their way back to the village."

At the average travel speed of a jonin, it was about thirty days from the village of Konohagakure to the Land of Redaku. Sasuke and Sakura would no doubt be a fair bit faster than that.

"Master Kakashi said he's going to stay a bit longer in the Land of Redaku," Shikamaru continued. "I guess he's backing the prince's coup d'état. We got that message from him a bit ago though, so it might already be over."

"The thing we got that petition for?"

About a week or so ago, Naruto had gotten a letter from the prince of Redaku asking for support with food. He'd already gotten a message from Kakashi that he wanted Naruto to help, so he promised his support, but he hadn't known that the situation had developed into a coup.

"Apparently, the new queen's reign is not going so hot," Shikamaru said. "People are starving to death."

As soon as he heard this, Naruto's face grew dark. Naturally, he wanted to do something. But if he carelessly interfered in another nation's civil war, he would create a pretext for them to invade the Land of Fire. It was hard to imagine that the battle power of the Land of Fire could be weaker than that of the Land of Redaku, but win or lose, he had no interest in waging war.

"We sure it's okay that Master Kakashi's supporting this coup?" he asked.

"Well, depending on how you look at it, it is interfering in another country's domestic affairs. The country's been closed off for a long time, and it's iffy whether this interference is valid." Shikamaru played with the long beard on his chin.

"As a Konoha ninja, there's no issue with him purging any rogue shinobi Redaku hired. But direct attacks on noncombatants like the queen and the prime minister are completely out of bounds. But, you know, there are other ways to handle it. Like, you make sure they attack first, and then all *your* attacks are under the guise of legitimate self-defense. It's Master Kakashi—he'll handle it right. Either way, our only means of contact is by hawk. It's no wonder you're worried."

"Right?!" Naruto said in a bright tone, trying to shake off his unease. There was a tight smile on his face.

Wears his feelings on his sleeve like always.

Shikamaru grinned and patted Naruto on the back.

"It's about time for you to get to work. Pretty much all of those proposals need to be done by the end of the week. Look them over sooner rather than later."

Three days later an unexpected guest paid Naruto a visit.

"There's someone here who says they want to see the Lord Hokage." The look on Moegi's face was clearly troubled as she announced this visitor.

Naruto and Shikamaru, who had their heads pressed together discussing the plan for the next year's railway construction, cocked their heads to one side, baffled. There were no appointments that day.

"She insists she's from the research institute, but she doesn't have any identification," Moegi continued. "Should I let her in?"

"What's it about?" Naruto asked.

"Err," Moegi stammered. "Some substance called, um, ultra particulate?"

Naruto and Shikamaru looked at each other.

"Let her in."

They had asked the institute to examine the ultra particles Sasuke and Sakura brought back. Naruto and Shikamaru waited nervously for this visitor, wondering if the analysis had been completed, but the timid figure Moegi showed in was Chihare.

"Um, the truth is," Chihare started after waiting for the sound of Moegi's footsteps to fade away. "I've found a way to cure your illness."

Shikamaru's eyes flew open, and then he frowned and looked at Naruto. He clearly was asking how this woman knew about Naruto's illness, but this wasn't the time for explanations.

"Really?!" Naruto leaped up, knocking his chair aside.

Chihare nodded. "At Director Furieh's request, I carried out an analysis of this new substance called 'ultra particles.' As a result, I found that the ultra particles have the effect of amplifying chakra."

"They amplify chakra?" Shikamaru said. "Then if someone who's no longer making chakra touches it..."

"My hypothesis is that the chakra flowing through the body's chakra channels will increase dramatically. If the Lord Seventh's illness is a type of poor functioning of the chakra channels due to taking a Biju into the body, then touching the ultra particles might improve the flow of the chakra channels. However." Chihare faltered and her expression grew dark. "The ultra particles likely belong to the institute, so they can't be readily moved. They're top secret. I shouldn't even be here leaking this information to you. If the Hokage were to negotiate directly, they might cede them to you, but this being Director Furieh, regular methods are—"

"Oh!" Naruto interjected. "No, we sent the particles to them for analysis."

Chihare raised her lowered eyes. "What?"

"It was our friends who found the ultra particles," he explained. "We handed them over to the institute and asked them to analyze them, but at some point, we'll get them back."

Chihare was silent for a full ten seconds, and then she said, deflated, "What? That's great."

"Thanks," Naruto said, smiling. Chihare had broken the rules to come here, not knowing that Naruto and his office were the owners of the ultra particles. For him.

"The fact that you analyzed the ultra particles," Shikamaru said with a probing glance. "Does that mean you were able to remove the wards on the vessel?"

"Wards?" she asked in reply. "By the time I got them, it was just the particles."

So had the institute removed the wards plastered all over the bamboo vessel?

"Where are the ultra particles now?" Shikamaru asked. "Do you still have them?"

"No." Chihare shook her head. "I handed them over to a messenger from the institute this morning. I think Director Furieh should have them now. They're quite unstable, so I'm sure he'll be doing a bit more detailed analysis in order to learn the best way to handle them."

"They're that unstable?" Shikamaru said, and Chihare nodded.

"They're extremely susceptible to water. A drop of water causes them to disintegrate. And they significantly amplify chakra, so for someone with a great deal of chakra, they're essentially poisonous. Touching them would double the amount of chakra in the body in an instant, and the keirakukei network would be destroyed."

Shikamaru thought for a moment. If there was a possibility that touching the ultra particles would cure Naruto's illness, then it was best to try it sooner rather than later.

"We need to come up with a reason to get the ultra particles back from the institute right away. I'll try getting in touch with Shizune," he said, and no sooner had he left the room than he hurried back and poked his face in. "Naruto. I forgot to tell you. Those proposals I gave you before, go over them by tomorrow."

He left the Hokage's office for real this time.

He's such a busy person.

Chihare looked around the Hokage's office once more.

The room was filled with papers. The rubber seal with "Seventh Hokage" carved into it sitting on one edge of the desk was already worn down, despite the fact that it hadn't been that many years since Naruto took office. In the garbage can were empty energy drink cans and several red pens that had run dry.

When she thought about the fact that *this* was the office of the Hokage, the leader of the village of Konohagakure, she felt sad somehow.

"Thanks, Chihare." Unaware of her sympathizing with the state of his office, Naruto flashed a grin at her. "You telling me right away about the ultra particles and potential cure has seriously taken a load off my mind. Believe it."

"I'm the one who should be thanking you," Chihare said, and just as she'd feared, Naruto's face went blank.

The clear blue eyes of the hero who'd secretly safeguarded the lives of so many people. He really didn't understand that the reason the scientists of the Five Great Nations were able to pour themselves into their research was because he had ended the Great Ninja Wars.

Chihare was going to be twenty-five that year. She had been alive at the time of Pain's attack and the Fourth Great Ninja War, and she had been very much self-aware, but she remembered hardly anything from those events. She felt like she had a hazy memory of her parents evacuating and taking her off somewhere. But no, maybe that had been just a regular trip? That was about the extent of it. As an adult, she had seen TV shows and magazine special issues looking back on this time period, and that was when she first learned how serious the situation had been.

She'd been kept safe. She hadn't known.

While the Five Great Nations fought and the shinobi protected the villages with their lives, Chihare had been at home, disassembling light bulbs and reading science books, and doing whatever she pleased. She hadn't even imagined in her wildest dreams that she was alive because someone was out there fighting for her. She was sure most children of her generation had the same perception.

"I don't know very much about the shinobi," she started slowly. "But I know that there are two human beings among them who are head and shoulders above all others at present. You're one of them, and the other is Uchiha Sasuke. The fact that you both desired peace is a major reason why the Five Great Nations were able to stop fighting. Because there isn't a shinobi who could beat the two of you in a real fight. The Sixth Hokage focused his efforts on developing the economy instead of the military and worked for the stability of the Five Great Nations, but he could only do that because he had you backing him up. By skillfully maneuvering and making good use of your strength as a deterrent to war, Hatake Kakashi built the peace we have now."

Although he didn't really take in her comments about him, when she spoke of Kakashi, Naruto nodded proudly. "That's right. Master Kakashi might look all spaced out, but he's seriously super amazing!"

Chihare stared hard at Naruto. *What I'm trying to say is that you're* more *amazing. This man only ever thinks of other people.*

"Before the Sixth Hokage came into power, chakra was for a long time used as nothing more than a tool of war. In that era, protecting the country was prioritized above all else. But it's different now. We scientists are able to devote ourselves to the research *we* want to do. The results of our work are measured against a standard for purposes other than war and evaluated properly. That is because you and your comrades created a peaceful society. Many scientists are grateful to you."

"Yeah?" Naruto awkwardly scratched at his face. "I feel like there aren't too many people who've thought that much about it though."

"At the very least, *I'm* grateful," she told him. "That's why I'm disillusioned by coming here today."

"Hm?" Naruto stopped moving.

"Is this the Hokage you wanted to be?" Chihare looked around the cluttered mess of his office in frustration. "Working nonstop day in and day out, and what is it you even do? Glued to your desk, checking papers, stamping them with your seal. Aren't you the hero of the Great War? Do you really enjoy doing this boring work?"

"Huh? Of course I do."

"Right, of course you—what?" So casually rebuffed, it took her a moment to hear what he said.

Naruto neatly pulled a tea caddy out from a haphazard-looking piles of papers and took a document out of it. "Here. Take a look at this. It's an order for headbands. For the kids who're graduating from the academy this year. I was super happy when I first put on my headband. So I get all excited just looking at this paper."

Chihare looked back and forth between the order form flapping in Naruto's hand and his happy face. "I think that this work doesn't need to be done by you in particular."

"I want to do it," he said simply and tucked the paper away before shifting his gaze to the photos of the successive Hokages hanging on the wall. "After Old Lady Tsunade became Hokage, her first job was to treat shinobi injured in battle. When Master Kakashi became Hokage, his was to hold the ceremony commemorating the anniversary of those who died in the Great Ninja War. With the Fourth... I dunno what his first job was, but with the era being what it was, I'm pretty sure he had plenty of unpleasant work."

The Namikaze Minato in the photo was looking straight ahead with a cool expression on his face, brimming with strength of will. But his eyes looked strangely gentle, like sunlight filtered through the leaves of a tree.

"And the first thing *I* did when I became Hokage was give a business license to a traditional sweet shop in the old city.

Makes you laugh, right? That's peace." Naruto chuckled and flashed a toothy smile at her. "Makes me happy that this is the kind of village we are now. Sometimes, I think I'm not cut out for desk work... But if my work can be food for the next generation like Boruto and Himawari, then I'm all in. As long as I can keep protecting this village, I don't care what form that protection takes. Some people call me a hero, but there's nothing better than no war at all."

A first-rate smile, brimming with strength of will. This smile had no doubt moved the hearts of many people. There was an endless power in his grin. It made you feel like wherever he was going, you wanted to go with him.

Maybe my understanding was mistaken, Chihare thought. *Maybe the reason he was chosen to be Hokage wasn't because he's strong.*

"You." She slowly looked at Naruto. "Why did you want to be Hokage?"

"I wanted people to accept me."

The answer was immediate. And unexpected.

He wanted people to accept him?

"That's not an answer," she said. "The way you are, people would still gather around you, even if you hadn't become Hokage."

"Huh? That's totally not true." Naruto blinked rapidly. Her words completely perplexed him. "You said that before, right? That stuff about me growing up loved... But actually, when I was a kid, I was always alone. Shikamaru, Kiba, and them were there when I was at the academy, but when I went home, there was no one. And just walking around the village, I'd get people tsking at me. Or a grown-up'd suddenly kick me. Anyway, people totally hated me."

"Liar," she said immediately.

"It's true," he said and opened a drawer. "I don't know if that's why, but either way, I wanted someone to accept me. That was what first got me wanting to be Hokage."

He pulled a brand-new headband out of the drawer and tossed it to Chihare, smiling proudly. "Take a look at that. The new headbands for academy graduates! The maker brought me a sample. They made some improvements to the material. They're lighter and tougher than last year's. So bright and shiny, huh?"

"Yes." Chihare traced the mark of Konoha engraved into the headband. The pattern of a swirling whirlpool was the symbol of this village. "You really do like people, hm?"

Naruto thrust his chest out. "Yup!"

•

"Nothing today either. No change at all! Believe it!" Naruto leaped down from the shelves, took off the goggles, and rubbed his temples. He'd mostly gotten used to using the Byakugan, but when he got carried away and used it for hours on end, his eyes grew exhausted, and it became hard to focus on anything.

They made no progress again that day. He didn't know how many tens of thousands of petri dishes he'd checked since he started working with Chihare, but they just couldn't seem to get any positive results.

"Have the ultra particles been returned from the institute yet?" Chihare asked, as she tapped away at the computer on the low table.

"Not yet!" His voice was rough with obvious dissatisfaction. "Shikamaru's pushed them to hurry, but they just give excuses about how they melt like sugar in water, so we have to do this and this, and then they never give them back!"

"Because it's an unknown substance. They probably want to keep it as long as they can to study it."

No change, no change, no change... After she copied and pasted the results, Chihare lifted her face up. "Anyway, where on earth did your comrades find such an unusual substance?"

"Oh," Naruto said. "This country called the Land of Redaku, waaaaaaay far to the west of the Land of Fire."

"The Land of Redaku, hm? That name does take me back."

Without warning, the two-person conversation increased by one.

Chihare gasped and whirled around to find Orochimaru standing there. He extended his long tongue and picked up the binder she had dropped in her surprise.

"This is our equipment, yes?" he said archly. "Could you take better care of it?"

"Orochimaru, you've been to the Land of Redaku?" Naruto asked, looking at the snake man with surprise.

"Yes," he said easily. "When I heard they had a forbidden jutsu that resembled Edotensei, I went to investigate. Although that was quite some time ago now. I made those goggles you're wearing by applying a technology I discovered in Redaku, you know."

The tip of his extended tongue flicked around the lenses of the goggles. Naruto pulled back, disturbed, and the corners of Orochimaru's mouth turned up.

"The jutsu that had been passed down in the Land of Redaku transplanted the power of someone else's eye. There's a legend that the Sage of Six Paths produced it for the sake of his blind friend Jean-Marc Tatar. Normally, the jutsu uses a prosthetic eye as the medium for giving the power of sight to a person who cannot see, but I applied it to goggles. They're still a prototype, but I'm glad they are proving helpful in the girl's experiment." Orochimaru shifted his gaze to Chihare. She shrank back and clutched the binder to her chest. "Although, well, it looks like that's not going too well."

"It's not." Naruto nodded and crossed his arms. "She's doing all this stuff every day, but the results just aren't coming in."

"It's a difficult thing to give birth to a new technology,"

Orochimaru remarked. "At any rate, all you can do is try and then learn from the failures. That's how Edotensei was born."

"Enough out of you." Naruto glared at him. "Don't lump her work in with a forbidden jutsu."

Orochimaru grinned happily.

"If you're using them every day, you must be getting a handle on the goggles. In three days, I'll have you show me just how much control you've gained over the Byakugan," he said and then shimmered abruptly like a mirage and melted into the air. He was as puzzling as ever.

Naruto's initial promise to Chihare had been to check for increases or decreases in chakra, but he always helped clean up before heading out. He discarded the special tanks for liquid chakra and washed the petri dishes with cleaning fluid.

"Hey, Chihare?" he asked. "You left the research institute because you wanted to, right?"

Chihare was getting ready for the next day's tests, and she looked back at him with the syringe to inject liquid chakra in one hand. "Yes, I did."

"Why'd you do that?" he asked casually, and Chihare was silent for a moment before answering.

"I told you before, didn't I?" she said finally. "I find other people stressful."

"That can't be all of it," he prodded.

"Why do you think that?"

"I mean, this experiment you're doing, in the end, it's for the sake of other people, right?"

Chihare paused and looked intently at Naruto's face.

Why is this person taking such an interest in me? From the perspective of the Seventh Hokage, I'm just a lone scientist, not even worth sparing a thought for. He has so many prestigious, well-known friends throughout the village, so why does he want to know about me?

She was confident that her experiment held significant meaning for the world and that it merited the cooperation of the Seventh Hokage. But Naruto's way of engaging with Chihare herself, the person running the experiment, was a complete mystery to her.

Is he like this with everyone? He is like this with everyone, isn't he?

"I found a star," she said.

"A star?" he repeated.

Her back still turned to Naruto, Chihare slowly began to speak. "I told you before that my field is astrophysics, right? About six months ago, I was observing the sky, and I found a star moving irregularly. From north to south, south to north— with each cycle, its trajectory changed slightly as it went around this planet."

"You mean like the moon?" Naruto asked.

"It was much faster than the moon."

The liquid chakra that dropped from her syringe landed squarely in the center of the petri dish. A twisted circle with just a bit of a tail. Almost like a falling meteor.

"I reported the existence of the star to the institute. But no one believed me. They said there couldn't be a heavenly body like that. They said it was impossible for it to be going round and changing its orbit at the same time."

"Couldn't you have just made them look at it?" he said. "Can't very well deny what they see with their own eyes."

"There are no researchers at Kengakuin with the skill to observe this star," she told him. "That facility is a place to do scientific research that will be 'useful to people.' Even if they had looked into the star, nothing would have happened. So management pressed me to give up astronomical research and move to a field that would lead to more practical results. I agreed and left the institute."

As she spoke, she grew more and more embarrassed. It felt like such an incredibly small thing when she explained it all again now. She'd left in a huff—like a child—because people didn't believe the star she'd found existed. Here she was saying that she wasn't good at working with other people, but in the end hadn't she wanted someone to recognize her efforts?

Wondering if Naruto was exasperated with her, Chihare looked at his face and found him nodding vigorously.

"Makes sense," he said. "That'd be a shock all right."

"..."

"I mean, if it were me, I'd super hate it. This thing really exists, and these people are all saying no, it doesn't. Just because it shouldn't."

"Well, that's all over now, so." Chihare felt a prickle in her nose and forcibly ended the conversation.

She relaxed when she was with him. He had a mysterious magnetism that she instinctively wanted to move toward, like being drawn to a sunny spot on a cold winter's day.

She moved to one end of the shelves as if running away and kept working.

A few minutes later, Naruto stuck his face in between the shelves, drops of water falling from his wet hands. "I washed all the petri dishes. What should I do now?"

"Oh... Please dry them."

"Yup." He slipped through the shelves and headed toward the drying room when suddenly the sound of his footfalls stopped. "Hey, Chihare? What's on this shelf here?"

"The petri dishes I just prepared," she said absently. "I think it'll still be a while before there are any results there."

"But there are," he told her.

"What?" She craned her neck.

"See? There. Chakra's seriously overflowing. Like water on dry ice." Naruto's finger was pointing to the top of a shelf, but Chihare's eyes could see nothing.

She moved over to the shelf to get a better look when she heard the sound of glass breaking in her breast pocket.

"What..."

The scouter she used to measure the amount of chakra had cracked. Wondering why, she turned to get her spare, and then rethought the situation and stopped.

It can't be.

She checked the cracked scouter once more and found that the needle had shot up to the maximum value. She looked at Naruto, then at the scouter, then up at the shelf before turning back to Naruto once more.

"What...?" She hesitantly brought the cracked scouter toward the shelf, and the overwrought needle snapped off at the base.

There was no mistake. Gaseous chakra filled the area around the shelf. An incredible amount of it.

"This is the first time," Chihare squeezed out, her voice almost shaking, "I've gotten a result."

"Yahoooooo!" Naruto scrunched up his face like a child and threw a fist into the air.

Insisting that they had to go grab a bite to celebrate this exciting progress, Naruto brought Chihare to a small food cart with a lantern hanging from it that said "Ichiraku." It was apparently a branch of a long-established ramen shop in the old city.

"When something good happens, you gotta have ramen," he told her. "Usually."

She didn't know what "usually" meant, but it was a pretty ordinary dining experience for the Seventh Hokage. The curtains hanging around the seating area were inherited from the main branch after its renovation and were quite dirty, stained with oil. On top of that, in this day and age, the place was powered with propane gas of all things.

Four of the mere six seats at the counter were already occupied. The eyes of the child sitting in the middle grew wide as soon as he saw Naruto's face.

"Ah! Dad!"

"Oh hey, Boruto. You're here too?"

Boruto, Mitsuki, Sarada. And the principal of the academy, Iruka, was sitting alongside them.

"Right now, Sarada's staying at Master Iruka's place," Boruto explained. "So we tagged along with them to Ichiraku."

"Lucky you. Getting Master Iruka to buy you dinner all the time," Naruto joked.

Iruka turned exasperated eyes on him. "Listen, you..."

Thoughtfully, the children shifted seats before Naruto had the chance to stop them, so Naruto and Chihare sat down in the two now-empty seats in the middle. From the left, it was Iruka, Naruto, Chihare, Boruto, Sarada, and Mitsuki—four generations sitting in order of age without anyone planning it.

"Brings back memories seeing you two sitting next to each other." Teuchi, on loan from the main branch, lowered his eyebrows happily as he set bowls of ramen out on the counter. "Aah. Master Iruka, you used to always bring Naruto with you back when he was a student at the academy."

"I still totally remember the first time Master Iruka brought me to Ichiraku," Naruto said. "After class, okay? He would always treat us to ramen. I was shocked to find that ramen this good even existed."

Iruka laughed fondly as he broke apart his wooden chopsticks. "Your eyes got so huge. You said something like 'this is *nothing* like instant ramen.'"

"Yeah. Ichiraku ramen's the best in the world! Believe it!" Naruto cried.

The ramen the *Seventh Hokage's head over heels about...*

Chihare scooped up the clear brown soup with a ramen spoon and looked at it intently. Sure that it was bound to be incredibly flavorful, she plunged her chopsticks into the noodles in the soup and lifted them to her lips. She unconsciously cocked her head to one side. Sure, yes, it was good, but...it was just regular ramen. Although it did warm her up. "Is it really *that* good..."

She hadn't meant her words for anyone else, but Boruto next to her heard her.

"Right?" he agreed in a voice quiet enough that Naruto and Iruka chatting with Teuchi couldn't hear, and lowered his voice even further before continuing. "But Dad and Master Iruka both love Ichiraku. I think Thunder Burger in the new city's way more delicious, hands down."

He glanced over at Naruto. "Don't tell Dad though," he added and slurped his ramen. For all his talk about hamburgers tasting better, he looked pretty happy with his ramen.

Chihare stared at the profile of the man seated next to her.

Naruto was laughing out loud, guilelessly, at Teuchi's cringey dad jokes, and the corners of his mouth turned up on his face with each slurp of his noodles, like he was in heaven. Every time the master next to him said something, he responded happily with laughter or anger or some other emotion.

Naruto almost certainly loved this ramen because of the nostalgia from his visits to this ramen shop with his teacher. They came here together after class, talked about all kinds of things, and had a good time, and he ended up associating all that with the ramen itself.

Now that she was thinking about it, Mitsuki had said something the other day about Boruto stopping off at the hamburger shop. She was sure that in Boruto's case, it wasn't a ramen shop, but a hamburger place. He killed time there with his friends, making fun memories, and so he liked burgers more than ramen.

I don't have a favorite food.

Chihare poked at the naruto-style kamaboko slice on top of her noodles. The fish loaf had a swirl in the center.

There were always so many people around Naruto.

"It's the perfect name for you. Uzumaki Naruto. Whirlpool," she murmured, and Naruto turned a happy face her way.

"Yeah! I like it too. Naruto kamaboko's delicious, after all."

"Not that part, your surname," she said. "There are whirlpool galaxies in space, you know. The theory is they have black holes at their centers that suck in all the material in the area. When water gets pulled into a gutter, it swirls around and around, right?"

Iruka stopped moving his chopsticks and looked at Chihare as she started lecturing about space.

"The center of the whirlpool never fails to pull in the things around it. It's all drawn in, creating a single large swirling move-ment. That really is you to a T. You seduce people with your overwhelming power of attraction."

"S-seduce? I feel like that's not really a compliment," Naruto scratched his cheek, troubled, and then shook it off and said, "But thanks. Uzumaki's my mom's surname. I only talked to her a little, but she was quite loud and strong and really like a black hole. Although her hair was red, not black."

"Kushina was a powerful person, I guess. They say she was always at the center of some sort of commotion, just like you," Iruka said with a faraway look in his eyes while he picked up the naruto kamaboko slice in his own bowl of ramen. "The 'uzuma-ki' whirlpool mark is also a symbol of Konoha. It honestly is the perfect last name for you."

Now that Iruka mentioned it, the whirlpool mark was also on the headbands the shinobi wore. Chihare looked at the one on Boruto sitting next to her and asked, "Why is the mark of Konoha a glyph like this? Also, it doesn't look much like a leaf."

"They say it comes from how ninja put a leaf on their forehead and trained to concentrate their chakra there," Iruka explained. "And the whirlpool imagery is from following its swirl from its edge until you eventually end up at the one point in the center."

"It does have that image of pulling together scattered things to a single place, doesn't it?" Chihare remarked.

"Mm hmm. But if you change the vector, it can also hold the opposite idea."

"Vector?" Naruto looked at Iruka curiously.

"If you come at it from the outside, you go *to* the central point," he replied. "But what happens if you do the opposite and trace it *from* the central point? You head toward the outside and continue endlessly. It changes into something that not only doesn't come together in one place, but scatters out eternally. The whirlpool is one of the few glyphs that expresses movement from inside to outside, and outside to inside at the same time. That's why in some of the country, it's a symbol of bonds. You could also put it like 'inside' is yourself and 'outside' is your friends."

As she listened to Iruka's instructional explanation, Chihare dropped her gaze to her bowl and the pink whirlpool on the slice of kamaboko.

"But the spinning has all kinds of different meanings, y'know!" Boruto interjected smugly. "If you look real close at sunflower seeds or cactus spines, they're in this pattern like a whirlpool. I guess it's so they can all get the same amount of sunlight."

"It's also a shape that's efficient for storing long things,"

Mitsuki noted. "My parent also sometimes coils up. When he's in snake mode and stuff."

"In some regions, they carve whirlpools into gravestones," Sarada said. "The constantly turning whirlpool is a symbol of eternity, so it's supposed to represent the hope that the dead person will come back at some point."

This was all new information to Naruto, and he was still for a moment, chopsticks in hand. "You kids really do study hard, huh?" he said finally.

"Did you learn all this, Dad?" Boruto asked. "At the academy?"

"I feel like we didn't really learn all these details back in my day," Naruto tried to deflect the question, and Iruka slapped him jocularly on the back.

"You dodo, I definitely taught them to you," he said firmly. "You just weren't listening because you were playing tic-tac-toe in the margins of your notebook with Kiba and Shikamaru."

"I can't believe you remember that," Naruto said, stunned.

Teuchi lifted his face as he put the plastic-wrapped chashu pork into the fridge. "Hey, hey. Sorry to interrupt your lively conversation, but you need to eat those noodles before they get gluey."

•

Chihare's research was finally coming to a close.

What kind of stimuli would have an effect on chakra in what kind of situation? Now that she had one answer to this question, she could do multiple regression analysis and get a rough idea of where to go next. The stage of testing blindly was over. The rest was logic, now that she'd made it this far.

She completed the prototype for her pluripotent applicator just three days after Naruto found the increased chakra with the Byakugan.

"A messenger from the institute is supposed to come this af-ternoon to pick up the prototype," she said to Naruto when she went to his office to make her report. "So the experiment is over for the time being. Thank you so much for all of your help."

"Same here," he replied, grinning from ear-to-ear. "I just know your research is going to help the people of Konoha. Thanks for all your hard work!"

Chihare awkwardly averted her eyes. Even now at the end of it all, she still wasn't used to how dazzling this person was. She left the Hokage's office with a peculiar feeling of regret.

That afternoon.

As promised, Naruto met up with Orochimaru on the cliff of Hokage Rock. He was there to show him his proficiency with the Byakugan while wearing the goggles.

"I suppose you've managed to master it somewhat then?" Orochimaru said.

"Never underestimate the Hokage!" Naruto replied enthu-siastically and snapped the band of the goggles on around his temples.

Of course, his expertise was still a long way from that of Hinata and Hanabi. But he was more than able to identify the chakra of people close to him and grasp his surroundings with-in a range of three hundred feet or so. Helping with Chihare's experiment and using the goggles every day was a big part of why he'd been able to reach this level of skill.

Orochimaru turned to Naruto, grabbed the goggles on his forehead, and slid them down over Naruto's eyes. He pulled the lever himself to turn the Byakugan on and stared at the blue eyes through the lenses.

"Tell me what part of my body I'm concentrating my chakra in," he instructed.

"Right hand." Naruto replied immediately, and Orochimaru's long tongue happily flicked out from between his thin lips.

"All right, how about now?"

"Left foot?"

"Now?"

"Mm... Right elbow?"

"Okay. Now?"

"Chin."

Each time Naruto got it right, Orochimaru's yellow eyes turned up, approaching the shape of crescent moons, until finally, the look on his face was an obvious grin.

"That's good sensing," he told the Hokage.

"Well, thanks." Naruto knew that was supposed to be a compliment, but it was creepy somehow. He scowled and then abruptly sensed a strong chakra outside of the village, so he turned his face in that direction.

"...!"

This chakra. It was Sasuke and Sakura. From the speed it was moving, they appeared to be using Susano'o. Kakashi had also returned safely to Konohagakure the previous day, so this meant that everyone would soon be back from the Land of Redaku.

That's great. Everyone made it home safely.

"What? What is it?" Orochimaru furrowed his brow doubtfully as he watched the sudden change in Naruto's movement.

"Oh, no. Um. It's nothing!" Naruto said hurriedly, and as if to distract Orochimaru, he looked toward the old city.

He spotted a familiar silhouette standing next to the half-destroyed house with the camphor tree. Chihare. Seeing her reminded him that she had said she was handing over the prototype. And as he watched, two men in white lab coats, looking very much like scientists, walked up and called out to her.

"Hmm?" He squinted and focused on the movement of the men. Judging from their carriage and the amount of chakra, they were probably both shinobi. What was that about? Did that mean they were both scientists *and* shinobi?

One of the men approached Chihare, smiling. As soon as he accepted the attaché case from her, he threw a fist into her solar plexus.

"That guy!"

When Chihare doubled over, the other man threw a burlap sack over her head.

Naruto moved to jump down from the cliff, but one of Orochimaru's snakes wound its way around his ankles, causing him to pitch forward and slam face first into the rocky ledge.

"Orochimaru! What are you doing?!"

"I could ask you the same thing. I can't see the way you can, so you will have to explain to me what happened."

"Chihare's been abducted. It's the guys from Kengakuin!" Naruto said and pulled the snake away to try and jump once more.

This time, a large serpent wound itself around his stomach. He nearly fell, but managed to brace himself somehow.

"Get out of my way!" he said angrily as he plucked at the snake around his waist.

Only it wasn't a large serpent. It was Orochimaru. The scaly body was that of a snake, but the face was Orochimaru's.

"Eee..."

Creepy!

Naruto automatically let go, and a tongue stretched out to lick his open palm.

"Calm down," the snake said. "I'm telling you to give them a bit of rope here."

Come on.

"Chihare is a scientist. They won't kill her before they confirm that her blueprints are correct."

"And when will that be?!"

"Who knows? Maybe three days?" Orochimaru replied casually, and this time, Naruto managed to push him off and look out across the village for Chihare.

The two men were fleeing, leaping from roof to roof. This was clearly the movement of shinobi. One of the men had the bag with Chihare inside hoisted over his shoulder.

Orochimaru said she likely wouldn't be killed right away, but that was no guarantee. Naruto kicked at the ground to go after them, but the snake man interfered for a third time.

"If you try to move again, I'm going to kill you." Orochimaru stood blocking his way.

"Why?!" Naruto glared at him. "What's it to you?!"

"I also want that applicator. And when one goes up against a person whose true identity is unknown, one must pin down their hideout and exterminate them. Otherwise, there's no point. Calm yourself. This is very unbecoming behavior for the head of the village."

While they stood there glaring at each other, the men and Chihare were getting farther and farther away.

"Fiiiiiiiine! I'll just watch for now!" Naruto spat, giving up. "In exchange, you help me. We're killing our auras and going after them."

•

The men arrived at the airship depot on the outskirts of the new city. It was closed that day, and there wasn't a soul around.

The premises included an enormous hangar that housed the Land of Fire's airships and a research facility built in cooperation with Kengakuin. The two men went into the research facility.

"Hey. What are you doing?" Orochimaru hurried to stop Naruto from yanking open a window.

"What do you mean, what?" Naruto said. "We gotta get inside."

"If you waltz in through the window, an alarm will sound, and we will face a world of complications," Orochimaru said sharply, apparently a break-and-enter expert. "Have you never broken into an international facility before?"

Of course I haven't.

Naruto gave up on going in through the window and agreed that Orochimaru would hack the security system. When they went around to the entrance, the two men were just coming out. Without Chihare.

Naruto and Orochimaru exchanged a look and kicked at the ground at the same time.

"What'd you do with Chihare?" Naruto asked, pressing on their shoulders from behind so they couldn't see his face.

Both men threw their hands in the air without the least resistance.

"If you mean that researcher, she's on the twenty-seventh floor. Electromagnet laboratory, right by the emergency stairs."

"We're just hired hands. We don't even know anything about who the boss is."

"Thanks," Orochimaru said gently and bit each of the men's necks in turn.

Naruto hurried to catch their bodies as they swooned and fell. "Hey! You didn't kill them, right?!"

With the entry card they took from the men, Naruto and Orochimaru marched right through the security gate at the entrance and snuck into the research facility. The building doubled as the control tower and was thirty stories high, but the floors in the middle were deserted. Naruto and Orochimaru raced up the emergency stairs and flew into the electromagnet laboratory on the twenty-seventh floor.

"Lord Seventh!"

Chihare was sitting on the floor in the middle of the room. She wasn't tied up or restrained in any way. She looked just as she had when she'd been abducted, like she could run out at any moment.

"You can move, can't you?" Naruto asked. "So why aren't you escaping?"

"I *can't* move!"

"Huh?" He dropped his gaze and saw caltrops scattered on the floor, except in a neat circle around Chihare. They weren't the usual iron ones, but reddish-brown copper caltrops.

Wait, what? In this day and age, plain old caltrops?

"You just have to avoid the edges on these things—" Naruto lifted a foot to step into the room, and the caltrops leaped up. One shot out with a whistle and grazed his toes, so he hurriedly pulled his foot back. "Aungh?! What *are* they?!"

The caltrops began to fly around the room, whistling through the air. What he'd thought was a boring trap that could only hurt you if you stepped on one of the chunks of metal turned out to be a contraption that moved three-dimensionally when intruders were detected.

The sight of the copper-colored fragments whirling around in all directions was almost beautiful, like a meteor shower. Although if he carelessly stretched out even a finger, these hooked stars would strip the flesh from his bone.

"Right?! I can't move!" Chihare cried.

Apparently, the place where she was sitting was the only safe zone; no caltrops passed through it. Which meant that she was surrounded by a chaotic sphere of flying caltrops and was stuck exactly where she was.

"I'm all right," she said. "The two of you, please go to the hangar! Right away!"

"What's in the hangar?" Naruto shouted.

"Director Furieh lied to me!" she said. "He's going to use the pluripotent applicator to replicate the ultra particles and scatter them in the sky above Konoha!"

"The ultra particles?" Naruto raised his shoulders curiously. "Why would he do that?"

"To target the shinobi, yes?" Orochimaru noted in his husky voice. "Ultra particles are harmless to the average person, but for shinobi with the large amount of chakra they possess, it's essentially a powerful poison. If it touches them, the increased amount of chakra will block the chakra channels and bring about all kinds of damage."

"What?!" Naruto yelped. "That's not great. We gotta stop him!"

"Please hurry!" Chihare begged. "Furieh's already equipped the airship with the device!"

Naruto looked back at Orochimaru. "I'm guessing there'll be security at the hangar too. You go ahead of me and break in. I'll join up with you after I rescue Chihare."

Orochimaru looked at Naruto like he wanted to say something, but then turned silently and left.

Unable to hear their conversation, Chihare raised her voice and urged Naruto to hurry. "Lord Seventh! You have to go too! To the hangar!"

"After I get you out of here!" he replied. "I can't just leave you."

Chihare was stunned and froze with her mouth open. "That's... This is no time to be prioritizing me. And how are you going to get through this trap anyway?"

"Force my way through! A hundred or so of these little caltrops hitting me isn't gonna kill me."

Naruto was about to jump into the fray, and Chihare quickly stopped him. "Aaah! Stop! Stop!"

The Hokage getting seriously injured because of her was no joke.

"You absolutely can't do something so dangerous!"

"What? Then what's your suggestion?" Naruto pursed his lips together, dissatisfied.

"Please look for a magnet," she told him.

"A magnet?"

"There should be one somewhere nearby. This trap most likely uses eddy currents for the caltrops."

Naruto screwed up his face in doubt.

"When you bring a magnet close to a piece of metal, it generates a powerful magnetic field in a whirlpool structure!" she explained quickly. "Most likely, there's an enormous magnet somewhere in this room, and the power of the magnetic field is moving all of these caltrops!"

Eddy currents were also used in the airship braking systems. And this was an airship development lab. She was certain there was a device generating eddy currents with an enormous magnet somewhere. The fact that the caltrops were copper was likely because that metal was more easily influenced by magnetic fields than iron.

"The movement of the caltrops might seem random, but if you look closely, they're moving in several whirlpool formations!"

When he focused on the chaos with the Byakugan, he did indeed find a regularity in the chaotic movement. Eddies were generated in the four corners of the room, and the caltrops were all rotating in line with one of them. With exquisite spacing so that no caltrop hit another, they spun endlessly in place.

But.

While Naruto followed the movement of the caltrops with his eyes, he came to a conclusion. "Whirlpools... This movement isn't that."

Master Iruka had said that the glyph of the whirlpool scattered endlessly toward the outside. But the movement of the caltrops before him was just a circle. Nothing more than independent rings, not connected to anything. They were simply spinning in the same place like planets around a sun; they weren't going anywhere.

If the movement was that simple, then he should be able to see through it.

Naruto pulled the lever on the goggles again.

"W-what are you going to do?" Chihare said.

"I am actually going to force my way in."

"What?!" Her eyes flew open wide in surprise, but Naruto was nothing if not confident.

"It's okay. I probably won't get hurt."

Whatever else was going on, he had the Byakugan he'd borrowed from Hinata. He peeled back his eyelids and set his sights on a place where the caltrops were sparse. He watched for the right time, like entering a jump rope, and then kicked at the floor.

His body danced up into the air, and a prick of pain ripped through the top of his ear. Caltrop thorns stabbed the arm he had covering his face. But Naruto didn't flinch at this level of pain and ran in a straight line into the eye of the storm in the center of the room.

"Owww. I guess they did actually get me a bit." Naruto grinned ruefully as he looked himself over.

Chihare stared up at him, astonished. "Did you see through all of those caltrops?"

"If you pay attention to the whole and plan your next move, it's not too hard."

According to Neji at least, Naruto added in his mind, and hoisted Chihare up.

"What are you doing?" she said.

"What do you mean, what?" He raised an eyebrow at her. "We have to get out of here."

Chihare realized that he intended to head back via the same path and paled. "Please let me down! There's a safer way to break through!"

"You mean, the whole go find a magnet thing?" he asked. "But it's not like I'm gonna find one right away. We don't have time."

"There's another way! Maybe try listening until I'm done speaking. You're too quick to jump into action the moment you have a thought." Grumbling, Chihare slid out of Naruto's arms and looked around the room intently before suddenly asking him, "Can you break the floor?"

"Break?" he parroted.

"However you want. Punch it, kick it. Just so long as you make a crack in it."

Eddy currents occurred when a magnet approached a flat metal piece. In the case of this room, the floor of iron panels was performing the role of metal, so if they could deform the surface so it was no longer flat, the eddy current would disappear.

Obediently, Naruto slammed a fist into the floor as hard as he could.

Pok!

It didn't shatter the way it would have if Sakura had been the puncher, but a large crack did open up in the floor. As expected, the whizzing caltrops stopped abruptly and clattered to the floor.

"What..." Naruto said, like the wind had been knocked out of his sails. "So I didn't need to force my way across."

With the slower Chihare over his shoulder, Naruto took the stairs four at a time down and out of the building, and headed for the hangar.

"Oh, they got you here too." Chihare plucked out a caltrop stuck in his back and tossed it away as she let out a sigh, her view of the world upside down. "Honestly. Why should the Seventh Hokage get hurt on behalf of someone like me? It doesn't make sense. If news gets out, I'm going to be the one taking all the heat, aren't I? Why are you so nice? If you think that every single person is worth protecting like your friends, you are seriously mistaken."

She knew that he was being nice enough to carry her and everything, but she couldn't stop the protest from spilling out of her mouth.

"I can't connect with other people in the world the way you do. I want to lock myself away and just live doing whatever I want. I'm that sort of person, you know?"

She grumbled at his back, and at first, Naruto let it slide, but he gradually grew irritated.

"Aah, come on! Enough already! If you say you don't want to, I'm not gonna force you to connect with people or whatever, you know."

"But you and your friends, what you care about is connecting with people, right?" she replied. "I'm just not suited to that kind of thing."

"Which is why I'm not pressuring you to open up," he retorted. "Way back when, we had to work together for the sake of everyone in the village, but those days are over now. If you say you don't want to connect with people, then that's fine. It's a peaceful society, you can live like that just fine."

Chihare fell silent.

When he told her that she was fine the way she was, she felt frustrated. Like her bluff was called and heeded, and her feelings had lost their place to land.

Naruto raced down the steps, his breathing entirely even, and his voice suddenly grew gentler.

"So Hinata, the family she was born into is a pretty famous shinobi family, and the times being what they were, of course she became a shinobi too. But she was never the type for fighting people and taking on those battles. If she had been born now, I feel like she definitely would have picked a different job. And I'm sure a whole bunch of other people really didn't want to fight, but forced themselves to do it anyway. I always wanted to change it so they had a choice."

Whenever he talked about his wife, his voice softened.

Chihare sighed as she stared at his broad back. *His wife must be amazing. Not all twisted like me.*

"So I'm serious, you don't need to force yourself to connect with people. Do it if you end up feeling like that's what you want to do."

Thd!

He leaped down the last twelve stairs from the landing and reached the first floor from the twenty-seventh in the blink of an eye.

"Anyway, why would Furieh get you to develop this device?" he asked. "Wouldn't demand for Kizahashi gas drop once it's complete?"

"He probably plans to make the Land of Kizahashi a monopoly. After he uses the ultra particles to eliminate the shinobi of all the nations, the shinobi of his own nation can use their chakra and copy the gas to completely dominate the energy market."

"..."

Furieh's thinking was the perfect picture of selfishness and, viewed from the position of the Seventh Hokage, utterly unforgiveable.

Naruto didn't say anything, but his back became a little hotter.

There was an enormous shutter on the front of the hangar for the airships to come and go through. Next to it was a small gate where Orochimaru was waiting for them.

"You done with your hacking?" Naruto asked.

"Of course," Orochimaru assented calmly, and behind him, the shutter for the gate slowly opened, as if to say, "Welcome, please come in."

It was pitch black inside the hangar. The slightly metallic scent in the air was no doubt from the Kizahashi gas used as fuel. The twelve airships owned by the Land of Fire were quiet in the darkness, like animals sleeping in their dens.

Furieh was somewhere in one of those twelve ships. If he was in the same place as the pluripotent applicator, then there would be a chakra signal. Naruto was about to put on the goggles and look for it when behind him, he heard a familiar mechanical hum.

"Chihare, get back."

She didn't need him to tell her twice. Chihare jumped back and pressed herself against a wall like a gecko.

Their first meeting in a month. The drones with the four propellers.

"You again!" Not sounding particularly surprised, Naruto dropped down into a defensive posture. The fact that the machines were here now meant that it had indeed been Furieh who sent the drones to Chihare's underground lab. Was his goal to eliminate Naruto?

"Whaaat are they?" Orochimaru said, eyeing them dubiously. "Such sad little things."

"They probably all have different functions," Naruto replied. "The ones I know self-destruct and—"

Drones appeared one after the other from the depths of the hangar. It wasn't a matter of ten or twenty. There were a hundred of them, flocking together like birds as they slowly approached.

"And some of them use laser beams." Naruto sighed and stepped forward, as if to say they might as well get it over with.

He grabbed an arm and pulled the machine in to smash the central spherical body with an uppercut. Inside was precision machinery, after all. Hit it, destroy it.

Three.

The view through the Byakugan caught a digital display blinking immediately behind his head. Two. A bomb drone had started its countdown.

"Not good!" Naruto looked back just as the countdown changed to one and then stopped.

The machine dropped to the floor with *clang*. One of Orochimaru's snakes had its fangs in the round body.

The battle had started, slowly but surely.

Drones versus Naruto and Orochimaru. The two shinobi wouldn't lose in an even fight, but there were so many drones. A hundred machines, and all were equipped with their own individual capabilities, which made it hard to figure out how to handle them. Suicide bombers. Machines that shot laser beams. And—

"Wacha!"

Naruto heard a bizarre sneeze and whirled around to look at the source, stunned.

"Wacha! Wachon! Waaah chooooon!"

Face covered with the sleeve of his kimono, Orochimaru sneezed again and again, his head rocking back and forth like a fan at a heavy metal concert. At least one of the drones was emitting poison gas, and Orochimaru had apparently gotten a blast from it. The sneezing left him wide open, and laser beam muzzles stretched out in his direction.

"Chon! Kacha!"

Even amid his ceaseless sneezing, Orochimaru's reactions were as quick as ever, and he leaped back to the right. Although he avoided the laser beams with room to spare, a different drone was waiting in the spot where he landed and cut his shoulder with its propellers. It was likely nothing serious, but Orochimaru's eyes twisted in humiliation.

"A mere machine—kacha! Has injured me..."

Cursing it did nothing. The drones shot after Orochimaru as one, as if they'd all realized they had him on the run. A muzzle slithered out of one drone, and the explosion timer started counting down on another.

Orochimaru stared coolly at the drones around him, but his nose was still twitching. "Haah... Haah..."

The muzzle flashed red. The explosion timer reached one.

"Haah... Haaaaaaachoo!!"

Zsh! Zsh! Zsh! Zsh!

Snakes flew out from Orochimaru's mouth. Mandala of Endless Snakes Formation—his unique jutsu that allowed him to spew an incredible number of snakes from his mouth. Several hundreds of the reptiles covered the floor like a scaly carpet, slithering and twisting and leaping at the drones.

"Ah!" Surprised by the snakes crawling around underfoot, Naruto lifted a foot reflexively, and Orochimaru grabbed it tightly.

"I've had it," he declared.

"Huh?" Naruto said, stunned.

Still holding Naruto's ankle, Orochimaru tossed him straight into the air. Naruto sailed up the full five meters to the ceiling of the hangar and grabbed onto a sprinkler.

"Whoa! What are you doing, Orochimaru?!" he yelled, dangling from the ceiling.

"I'm done with this one-at-a-time situation. Go find the operator."

The operator. Of the drones.

They might have been running on a simple program, but considering the way the drones were working together and the timing of the initial explosion, it could be that someone was giving them instructions.

Chihare did *say that Furieh was in the hangar...*

Arm still hooked over the sprinkler, Naruto looked down on the enormous space.

The heated battle of Snakes versus Drones was unfolding all around. The snakes were making good use of their ropelike bodies to twist and turn and skillfully toy with the drones.

Having finally stopped sneezing, Orochimaru was smashing the drones closest to him one after another in annoyance.

Boom!

Naruto put on the goggles and examined the airships.

"There we go." He could sense chakra in the one parked by the north entrance, and he let go of the sprinkler.

Rather than simply falling in a straight line to the floor, he grabbed onto the arm of a passing drone. The captured machine shuddered and lost altitude, but surprisingly, it didn't crash. In fact, not only did it keep flying, it stretched out the muzzle of its gun in front of Naruto's nose.

Chk! The tip flashed red.

Perfect. Just as the gun was about to fire, Naruto twisted around and forcibly changed the drone's direction. He turned the tip of the muzzle toward the airship parked near the entrance. The whole maneuver took less than a tenth of a second.

The laser beam shot straight forward and hit the airship, just like Naruto had intended.

Boom!

The wooden wall swelled up, burned to ash, and blew outward with the top of the ship. Naruto leaped down from the drone and went inside the airship.

From the exterior, he'd assumed it was a three-floor passenger type, but the interior had been retrofitted so that it was a single enormous room. A man holding a laptop computer was crouched on the floor near the prow.

He had the same face as the one Naruto had seen on the

research institute's website. Kanhen Furieh.

"Sup." Naruto moved in a single leap to stand before Furieh. He tried to stay calm, but his voice betrayed his anger. "First time we've met in person, huh? Mr. Director Furieh."

"Eep!" Furieh squeaked and began to tremble. He was operating the drones with the computer he held in both arms.

He was the head of an international organization, but his reaction upon seeing Naruto was quite pitiable. Pale lips shaking, eyes swimming about, he was so pathetic that Naruto couldn't even muster up the energy to hate him.

"I don't want to be any more violent than I have to be," Naruto said flatly. "You get that, right?"

Furieh was scared. He shook his head up and down, opened the laptop, and tapped at the keys to deactivate the drones, which suddenly dropped to the floor outside the ship.

"Where's Chihare's device?"

With a frightened look on his face, Furieh raised a trembling finger.

Naruto followed it with his eyes and saw a black cube-shaped machine toward the rear of the ship's interior—the pluripotent applicator. A round flask was connected to the machine, and silver sand glinted and glittered inside the glass sphere.

Those are the ultra particles then?

Seeing Naruto turn his attention toward the device, Furieh pulled a photon gun from inside his jacket. Of course, Naruto reacted quickly and easily dodged it, but the laser beam hit the flask of the pluripotent applicator.

Bang!

Glass flew everywhere. The exposed ultra particles spilled out onto the floor.

"Furieh!"

Still the coward right up until the nth hour.

A second before Naruto's clenched fist shot out, a snake with its mouth wide open flew up to sink its fangs into Furieh's throat. Orochimaru's snake. The fangs were so deep in the administrator's flesh, they were without a doubt poisoned.

Mere seconds later, Furieh's eyes rolled back in his head, and he went quiet.

"You better not have killed him!" Naruto shouted, racing over to Furieh to check that he was still breathing. "Aah, that's something at least." He let out a sigh of relief.

"Don't worry. That one just happens to have a paralysis poison," Orochimaru said, shrugging slightly as he came into the airship.

"Great," Naruto replied. "We'll hand this guy over to the Anbu. He might have people working with him, but they'll get that out of him."

"What are you talking about? No point in letting a man like this live." Orochimaru scowled, picked up the photon gun on the floor, and pointed the barrel directly at Furieh. "Faster just to kill him."

"Stop!"

Before Orochimaru could pull the trigger, Naruto flew at him, and the two tumbled to the floor. After rolling along the ground several times, Naruto somehow managed to snatch the photon gun away from Orochimaru, but the snake man stretched out his tongue and wrapped it around the gun. They each pulled on it for a while, a bizarre tug of war.

"Just when I thought you'd mellowed a bit!" Naruto cried. "You never change, do you!"

"Heh! You're slipping. Could you not just go deciding things like that?" Orochimaru gave up on trying to win by force, pulled his tongue away, kicked at the floor, and got some distance from Naruto.

Wham!

Taking a vital hit, Naruto dropped the photon gun but immediately kicked it far away and stopped Orochimaru's fist with one hand. He then caught the snake man's other driving punch with his other hand.

The two fighters pushed against each other, and once again, it became a contest of strength.

"You're soft, hm?" Orochimaru cooed. "Letting the man who tried to assassinate you live!"

"Shut up!" Naruto grabbed onto the sleeve of Orochimaru's kimono and yanked him toward himself.

Konk!

Orochimaru took a headbutt right in the chin. Followed by two elbow strikes. Naruto had to finish this quickly with a close-range physical fight. It would all be over if Orochimaru managed to get some distance and weave some signs. Naruto obviously wouldn't stand a chance if he got dragged into a ninjutsu fight, not when he couldn't use chakra.

He launched a right straight at Orochimaru's slender jaw as if to strike the final blow, and Orochimaru clamped a hand around his wrist.

Yellow, reptilian eyes locked onto Naruto from between the gaps in the mess of long black hair. A chill ran up his spine, and when for a moment, Naruto couldn't move, Orochimaru's fist came down on his face.

"Mmph!"

His lip split with a resounding crack. He was punched twice, three times, and the blood flowing from his lip mixed with that from his nose and dripped onto the floor. Naruto was trying to keep ninjutsu from being used, and here Orochimaru was, proving to be a real opponent in a physical fight.

Right around the seventh punch, Naruto somehow grabbed onto Orochimaru's sleeve and yanked him hard down to the floor. He wrapped his arms around the other man's elbows and was about to try out some locking techniques when he heard a *whnk*. He dropped his gaze with a gasp and saw that Orochimaru's eyes had rolled back and he was foaming at the mouth. His dislocated right arm hung limply at his side like a mollusk.

Huh? But I didn't do anything yet!

While Naruto was distracted, Orochimaru slithered out of his arms.

"Ah!"

Right. This snake man could dislocate his joints at will. The frothing at the mouth had just been a distraction.

Orochimaru scooped up the photon gun and turned the barrel toward Furieh laid out on the floor.

Vuwm!

The laser beam shot out and grazed the director's knee.

"Aaaugh!" Furieh threw himself back. His knee bounced up at the touch of the super high-temperature beam and burst into flames. The heat moved from cell to cell, the fire growing larger before their eyes, spreading from knee to thigh to hip.

"Aunh! Hot! Ah! Aaaaaah! Aaaaaaah!"

Furieh writhed around on the floor in anguish, but that wasn't enough to put out the fire started by the photon gun. The roaring flames were already licking at his stomach.

"You!"

Naruto leaped at Orochimaru's back. The photon gun dropped from the other man's hand and clattered onto the floor. Naruto clenched a fist to finish this with a single blow, and Orochimaru suddenly vanished. Naruto whirled his head around as a hand stretched out from behind to grab his neck.

"Quite a misunderstanding to think that *I* had *mellowed*." Orochimaru's murmuring caressed his earlobe. "Killing Furieh, one man, is nothing to me."

"So then why...did you try! To stop Furieh...! I bet...it's be-cause...Mitsuki's in town!" Naruto panted, his windpipe crushed and his consciousness beginning to fade.

Something hit his heel. The photon gun Orochimaru had dropped.

Squinting to focus his blurred vision, he saw Chihare fear-fully pressed to the wall outside the airship.

"Chihare!" Naruto shouted, his voice on the verge of giving out entirely, and kicked the photon gun. It spun around as it slid across the floor and came to a stop when it hit Chihare's foot.

Orochimaru slowly turned his face toward her.

"Give that to me," he said in a low voice. He let go of Naruto and slowly walked toward Chihare.

"Chihare! Pick it up!" Naruto cried, mustering what was left of his hoarse voice, still on his knees. "Pick it up and fire at the ceiling!"

Chihare jumped at the photon gun, squeezed her eyes shut, and pointed the barrel at the ceiling.

Bang!

The spot where the beam of light from the muzzle hit was charred black in an instant, and the heat quickly spread through the entire ceiling.

"What are you..." Orochimaru muttered.

The hangar's sprinklers were heat-sensing types. If the system detected temperatures above a certain baseline, it would issue an order to the disaster prevention units set up at ten-yard intervals and put out the fire.

Silver devices popped out of the ceiling and water rushed out from them. Clouds rose up as the water evaporated, and the flames burning Furieh's body sizzled and died out.

The inside of the hangar was immediately flooded. The airships, the pluripotent applicator, and the ultra particles that spilled to the ground when the flask broke.

"…"

Naruto had known this would happen, which was why he told her to fire at the ceiling.

The ultra particles his friends had brought back for him evaporated in little puffs of white steam.

Chapter 4

"So to sum up." Sasuke had moved beyond bad mood and crossed over into fully enraged, as he sat cross-legged with his back against a beam. "You let the ultra particles disappear before your very eyes to save the life of your enemy?"

"Well...I guess so." Naruto scratched his cheek awkwardly.

He really was truly and sincerely sorry for destroying the ultra particles Sasuke and Sakura had worked so hard to get from far-off Redaku. But he felt like he hadn't had a choice. He couldn't let Furieh die.

The back room of Tami's sweet shop.

Chihare had been added to the usual lineup of attendees. When they heard the solemn news about the ultra particles' disappearance, they all dropped what they were doing to meet.

"Um, anyway, allow me to add," Chihare interjected tentatively, shrinking back at an already intimidating and suddenly scary Sasuke on her first meeting with him. "The Lord Seventh came to rescue me, and I was the one initially deceived by Furieh, so it's really—"

"I know that much," Sasuke interrupted. "You be quiet."

Thus rebuked, Chihare obediently fell silent.

The vein that had popped up on Sasuke's forehead showed no signs of settling down. He was outraged that the village chief Naruto would prioritize those around him over his own life.

"No use crying over spilt milk. We need to figure out our next step. We're out of time here," Sakura said, trying to pacify Sasuke and bringing them back to square one.

She had put together all the information each of them had brought back from the Land of Redaku, given Naruto another careful examination, and produced a hypothesis about his illness that she was fairly certain was accurate.

As she had initially suspected, taking a Biju into his body was the source of Naruto's malfunctioning chakra channels. There was likely no mistake about that.

Nine Tails' chakra only flowed through Naruto's body when Nine Tails made a decision to lend it to him. But in very rare cases, the repeated borrowing and lending of chakra could blur the boundary between the chakra belonging to Tailed Beast and chakra belonging to Jinchurikii, so that a minute amount of Tailed Beast chakra was continuously flowing through the body of the jinchuriki. As this continued, Naruto's own chakra channels increasingly viewed the Nine Tails' chakra as foreign to his body and attempted to get rid of it by narrowing and closing his chakra channels. Naruto's episodes were a side effect of his chakra channels forcibly contracting over and over.

"It's been two weeks already since your last episode, right?" Sakura asked, and Naruto nodded. "The ceasing of episodes proves that your chakra channels are closing up. If they close completely, they probably won't recover, not even with the ultra particles."

"How much time do we have until they close completely?" Sasuke asked.

"Judging from the results of this round of testing, I'd say

three days," she said, the look on her face stern.

Three days.

The blink of an eye. The lantern flame suddenly flickered in the windowless room, perhaps because someone let out the breath they were holding.

"There's still a way to get the ultra particles. There has to be," Shikamaru said, shifting his gaze from Sasuke to Sakura.

"Yes. The Sage of Six Paths split the ultra particles into two and hid them in 'the star that never strays' and 'the sky that fell to the earth.' We found the ultra particles sealed in 'the sky that fell to the earth,' so if we can figure out the location of 'the star that never strays,' we should be able to get the other half of the ultra particles." Sakura paused there, and her face grew dark.

Most likely, "the star that never strays" was also in the Land of Redaku, just like "the sky that fell to the earth." Even if they set out that very minute, Naruto's chakra channels would close up before they even neared the Land of Redaku.

"The last clue we have...is this piece of straw paper?" Shikamaru set out the paper with its fold lines on top of the tatami mat.

Chihare craned her neck forward and peered at it. "What is that?"

"Oh, is this the first time you've seen it?" Shikamaru asked. "It was wedged into *Map of the Heavens*. It's just this one line saying the stars increased. We have no idea what it means. But I'm more curious about the Konohagakure mark." He stroked the swirling mark in ink with the pad of his finger.

Until Kakashi sent his first letter, there was no direct communication between the Lands of Fire and Redaku. About all each country knew of the other was faint rumors and utterings from travelers and merchants about a distant country. Both countries doubted that the other actually existed, and yet the glyph that signified the village of Konohagakure was discovered on a piece of paper in the Land of Redaku. It was too strange.

"At the academy, Master Iruka taught us that the Konoha mark came from the tradition of shinobi who would train with a leaf on their forehead to focus their energy. Maybe this paper with the mark of Konoha on it means that the other half of the ultra particles is in the Land of Fire."

"That's probably wrong."

All eyes in the room focused on Chihare.

"The whirlpool motif is used in countries all over at all points in history. It's plenty possible a similar symbol would pop up somewhere else. In Konoha, the whirlpool is a mark that expresses concentration of energy, but in the Land of Redaku, it might have a completely different meaning."

"So then what would that different meaning be?" Shikamaru asked, annoyed, and Chihare looked directly at him.

"It was written in the ancient text, right? The Sage of Six Paths caught the meteor and split it. In which case, it could be that this drawing indicates the falling meteor, couldn't it?"

Meteor.

Sakura took off her headband and looked intently at the familiar symbol with fresh eyes. She could actually maybe see something like a falling meteor in it. The upside-down triangle at the bottom left could be interpreted as the path of the meteor.

"But there's something not quite right for a symbol of a meteor," she said.

"It's a whirlpool," Naruto interjected. "Orochimaru said so. In the Land of Redaku, the helix is a symbol of rebirth. But a meteor hasn't got anything to do with rebirth. Why draw something that only falls with a whirlpool?"

"True," Sakura murmured. "*Map of the Heavens* was clearly written to tell later generations the location of the ultra particles. They must have had a reason for deliberately adding the whirlpool."

"A reason?" Shikamaru put a hand to his chin and sank into thought.

Naruto stared at the piece of paper and then slowly opened his mouth. "Maybe the meteor was reborn?"

Chihare looked at Naruto.

"It didn't just fall and that was the end of it," he continued. "The Sage of Six Paths returned half of the meteor to the sky. Used a jutsu to keep it going round and round forever, never pulling away from the earth, like the moon."

Sakura and Shikamaru said nothing as they considered the possibility of what he was saying.

The idea that half of the ultra particles were orbiting the planet was absurd on its face. But Naruto was brimming with confidence, nevertheless.

Indeed, if it was going around the planet as a satellite, then the phrase "the star that never strays" suddenly made sense, and "the stars increased" also snapped into place. From the day the Sage of Six Paths launched the satellite, there would have been one more star in the night sky.

"Hmm," Sakura groaned, a complicated look on her face. "Say you're right. Then it would have to be fairly high up and moving completely differently from the other stars. That kind of celestial body—"

"Exists!" Chihare's voice suddenly rang out sharply in the small attic room. "That celestial body exists!"

A celestial body much faster than the moon, spinning around this planet.

She was sure of it. Chihare had observed such a celestial body with her own eyes any number of times.

"There's a body that passes through the sky directly above the Land of Fire in a fixed period. The orbit is 660,000 feet up. The next time it will be observable in Konohagakure is tomorrow night at ten p.m. If you miss that, you won't be able to see it again for six months," Chihare said all in one breath, her cheeks reddening with excitement, and she looked around at the assembled faces. "I did fairly detailed observations, so I can precisely identify the orbit."

"Do you have any records?" Sakura asked. "Maybe you could show them to us?"

"Of course. I'll go get them." Chihare shook her head up and down and flew out of the attic room, panting, to get her notes.

Naruto's theory took on a sudden flavor of truth.

The other half of the ultra particles was going around this planet without straying as a satellite. If this preposterous theory was true, then how on earth were they supposed to get ahold of them?

The whole group sank into thought.

"I'll build a pillar with Earth Style," Kakashi said, breaking his long silence. "Sakura, Sasuke. You two run up the pillar and carry Naruto to the top. You can make it if you use Chihare's system bike. Sakura'll be in charge of chakra control to ride up the vertical wall, and Sasuke will supply chakra to the engine."

"An Earth Style pillar 660,000 feet tall? Can you do that, Master Kakashi?" Sasuke asked him doubtfully.

"I'll have to," Kakashi said, his tone light, and he crossed his arms. "Although, my chakra might run out halfway through. Well! I've got an idea about who I can partner up with."

"So it's settled," Sasuke said firmly, and Shikamaru was forced to swallow the argument on the tip of his tongue. He was against this absurd plan.

For Shikamaru, who was the type to look both ways and then double check before he crossed the street, this plan was a nightmare come to life. But if Sasuke and Kakashi were on board, all that was left to do was carry it out.

He let out a long sigh and looked squarely at Sasuke. "Even if you do reach the satellite, how are you planning to undo the seal from there? The ultra particles' vessel is likely sealed with the same wards as the one in the lake."

"I'll smash it." Sasuke's response was simple.

"Seriously?" Shikamaru asked, incredulous.

"Of course," Sasuke answered evenly.

He's not going to bend now.

Shikamaru pressed a hand to his eyes with a bitter look on his face.

"I'll handle that."

"Right. Please and thank you."

It was settled.

The next night at ten p.m., the satellite would pass directly above the training ground. Before it did, Kakashi would make a pillar of earth shoot into the sky, and Sakura and Sasuke would ride the bike up the side of it.

Twenty-eight hours until mission start.

Now that everything had been decided, the group started to stand, and Naruto stopped them.

"Guys. So, like."

"What, loser?" Sasuke glared at him. "You're not actually hesitating about us helping you again, are you?"

"No. I'm okay with that." From where he sat cross-legged, Naruto put his hands on his knees and lowered his head. "Thanks. I'm super counting on all of you."

Kakashi and Sakura patted his shoulders from either side.

"The Hokage can't go bowing his head to just anyone." Shikamaru smiled wryly, and Naruto grinned with him.

He wasn't bowing to just anyone. He was bowing to *them*.

Chihare's observation records were impeccable, and Sakura and Shikamaru both gave them their seal of approval. There was no doubt that this star of hers was the Sage of Six Paths' satellite.

With everything sorted and settled, it was finally time to carry out the mission. They had to get moving as soon as possible to get ready.

It would be suspicious to have a group like them seen moving together as one, so the party left the shop one by one at carefully timed intervals. Naruto to the Hokage's office to get a jump on his normal work in preparation for tomorrow night. Shikamaru to make arrangements to "handle that." Kakashi to scout his "partner." Sakura with Chihare to practice riding the bike. And Sasuke—he had nothing in particular to do, so he decided to go home right away and conserve his strength.

"Sasuke."

He'd slipped through the back door and gone out into the alley, when a voice called out to him.

It was Hinata.

This wasn't the sort of place she would have just happened to be passing by. She couldn't have ambushed Sasuke here unless she knew that he and the others were meeting in the hidden room of Tami's sweet shop.

"What is it?" he asked.

"Thanks for all the things you do for Naruto."

Has she realized it then?

Sasuke hid his consternation and kept his face expressionless as he peered at her. Naruto was keeping his illness a secret from his family. If she'd long ago picked up on it and said nothing because she respected Naruto's feelings, she was one incredible wife.

"I've done nothing you should thank me for. I'm only doing what I want to do," Sasuke said coolly and walked past her.

Hinata lobbed something. "Here!"

Once he caught it, he realized it was a headband with the mark of Konoha.

"Better to have something to protect your forehead," she told him.

Sasuke stared at Hinata, a strange feeling coming over him.

He'd never been good with her. She was always so timid and had no confidence in herself despite being a hard worker. She made it seem like she had no opinions of her own, always watching other people's faces, looking for the right thing to say or do. He used to get annoyed whenever he saw her.

But during the time he'd been away from the village, Hinata had changed. Her core strength locked away inside of her reserved nature began to reveal itself. With that secret strength, she sometimes watched over Naruto, sometimes supported him—and before he knew it, she had married him.

"I'm not officially a Konoha shinobi. I can't wear—"

"Make sure to give it back," Hinata interrupted Sasuke as he was about to return the headband to her and turned sharp eyes on him. "I can't let my husband be responsible for your life too."

He really was uncomfortable with this woman.

The training ground, wrapped in the hazy red light of the setting sun.

At the request of Kakashi, Yamato dropped his duties monitoring Orochimaru in order to be Kakashi's partner and learn about the absurd mission to send a pillar 660,000 feet up into the air. He stood there with a look on his face like he'd been forced to eat a live caterpillar.

"And you're doing this tomorrow? You're as reckless as ever, hm, Kakashi?"

"Aah, I'm just glad I have such an excellent comrade here with me," Kakashi said. "That height, even I'll run out of chakra by the time it's halfway up."

"And there you go again. I'm getting on in years myself though, so I can't be swayed by flattery," Yamato retorted sharply, but his face relaxed into a smile. No matter how many years passed, he would always be happy to receive compliments from the older man he had long looked up to.

Kakashi might have teased him with flattery, but it was a simple fact that he relied on Yamato. He was the rare man who could quietly handle a difficult and dull job that never garnered him any true glory. Yamato's powerful abilities and his humble steadfastness had saved Kakashi any number of times.

"About 310,000 feet is the most I can do with my Wood Style and still produce something strong enough to handle the system bike riding up it," Yamato told him. "Even if I scrimp on the strength by half and combine with your Earth Style, Kakashi, I have my doubts about whether or not we could make it all the way to 660,000 feet."

"The issue isn't just the amount of chakra, hm?" Kakashi mused.

They wouldn't get anywhere unless they gave it a try.

The two shinobi stood facing each other in the center of the training ground.

They considered a variety of ways to link Earth and Wood Styles but decided in the end on Yamato first producing a support pillar of wood which would be coated by Kakashi's Earth Style. It was a combined ninjutsu that required fine chakra control and a precise combination.

"Oh, I'll just throw it out, so you match me, okay?" Kakashi said lightly.

"What?! ...I understand."

"No, no, kidding. We'll work together."

Yamato realized Kakashi was teasing him and frowned, looking not entirely displeased.

They made eye contact again and then both of them slapped a hand against the ground at the same time.

Bang!

Earth Style and Wood Style. Their two different chakras raced into the earth together.

Dwoom!

The thick trunk of a tree rose up first, a millisecond faster. Earth Style crackled as it covered the tree stretching up straight toward the heavens.

But the earth wrapping around the tree was shooting up a tiny bit faster than the tree was growing. Once the pillar reached a height of 32,000 feet, the earth wall surpassed the tree trunk, lost its supporting pillar, and crumbled back down.

"Aaah..."

It was already broken.

Yamato shrugged, eyes turned upward chasing after the tip of the extending pillar.

Well, the first attempt was always like this. Perfectly matching different ninjutsu normally required years of practice. Trying to complete this task in the span of a single night, no matter how skilled the two shinobi, was the absurdity Yamato was talking about.

"You're worried. I am too," Kakashi said in a light tone, perhaps guessing at Yamato's anxiety.

"There's nothing to do but try, right?" Yamato gave voice to the words he expected from Kakashi next. "It's for Naruto, after all."

After returning to the Hokage's office, Naruto checked the documents piled on his desk and split them up into separate piles. Papers he'd stamped his seal onto, papers that couldn't be processed for one reason or another, and papers he would talk with Shikamaru about before deciding anything. He wanted the first stack to grow, but unfortunately, the three mountains remained basically equal.

He lifted his gaze abruptly and met his own eyes in the window of his office. The glass, covered in a protective film, reflected the inside of the room less than it showed the outside, so he couldn't really see the scene on the other side.

I wish I could go outside.

Naruto looked over the mountains of documents in the glass and sighed deeply. He wanted to see the lights of the village. He wanted to sit on the rocky face of the Fourth Hokage in the middle of the seven faces and look down on the village. But he couldn't. He had to finish tomorrow's work tonight.

Tomorrow.

Tomorrow night, his friends would bring him to the spot where the satellite would come.

Maybe someone like you who grew up loved by the people around you can't understand that.

Chihare's words came back to life in his ears. He had denied them, but it was true that he was blessed. With friends. And talent.

Naruto stood and picked up the framed picture decorating his shelf. He took the back off and pulled out the other photo tucked away behind the photo of the four members of Team Kakashi.

In the faded sepia world, Minato and Kushina were walking alongside each other.

The photo had apparently been taken without their knowledge; neither of them had their eyes turned toward the camera. Kushina was talking happily, walking slightly ahead of Minato, red hair swinging, and Minato was smiling as he looked at her back.

Tsunade had given him this photo a long time ago. She'd found it among Jiraiya's things, but she didn't know who had taken it.

Standing there, Naruto stared at the faces of his parents, who were younger than he was now.

He had been bullied in the village and gained the power of Nine Tails' chakra because Minato had sealed the Nine Tails, Kurama, inside of him. Because of that, Naruto got to meet Kurama.

So then what if Kurama had never been inside of me?

"..."

He tightened his grip on the photo in his hand, and wrinkles popped up around his mother's face in profile.

He'd thought about this over and over since he learned that he might lose his chakra. Who exactly would he be with no chakra?

What if his father hadn't sealed Nine Tails inside of him? What if Naruto had never had Nine Tails' chakra? Would he still have been able to help his friends and fight his enemies? If he didn't have Nine Tails inside of him, he might not have become Hokage.

No, you're wrong, a low voice replied inside of his head. *Even if I wasn't here, you would have become Hokage. With your ninja path, never twisting your own words, and your impossible stubbornness, you would have pulled your comrades forward and saved your enemies. And the people would have accepted you and selected you as Hokage. It's me telling you this, so you know it's not wrong.*

"You're awake then?" Naruto said. "You've been doing nothing but sleeping lately."

Kurama sniffed indignantly. *You think these silly thoughts woke me? I will sleep again now.*

Naruto knew himself that it was silly. If he didn't have Kurama, his parents would have lived, and he would never have been bullied in the first place. The Great Ninja War might not even have happened, and this would be a completely different world. There was no point in even thinking about it.

There was no point, but...

"Hey, Kurama?" Naruto said, but either Kurama really had gone back to sleep or he was awake and ignoring Naruto. Either way, Naruto got no reply.

He thought about it over and over and over. What exactly would be left for him once Nine Tails' chakra was gone?

His mother had taught him the answer to that a long, long time ago. The love that Kushina and Minato poured into him had been in there all this time, and now, the new Team Seven, Shikamaru, his family, and everyone in the village filled him up with new feelings each and every day.

He'd trained so much and gained a variety of techniques and abilities. But to Naruto, his greatest strength was that he had good friends. He was proud of them from the bottom of his heart.

It's okay, Naruto told himself. *I'm sure they'll save me tomorrow.*

·

"Amazing, huh? It really does just keep on burning."

"It's like, this is way more Land of Fire than our actual Land of Fire, you know?"

The next day, Ino and Choji each offered up their thoughts looking down on the burning hill from the viewing platform of a commercial building. On the slope blanketed by faded vegetation were orange flames stretching up from inside the earth.

A modern cityscape spread out in the south stood in contrast to the simple fields that could be seen to the north. Buildings soared high like they were holding up the sky, and the walkways were covered in closely spaced tiles.

"Both of you, come on. We'll go over the plan," Shikamaru called, and Ino and Choji moved away from the glass window.

Sadly, the three members of Team Asuma had not taken several trains to the Land of Kizahashi to take in the views. Shikamaru had abruptly called them together the previous night and told them the details of what was going on, and soon they were on the night train bound for the Land of Kizahashi.

They had been surprised to learn Naruto was ill with a serious disease, but they had been more shocked by the details of the mission they'd been given. Sneaking into the Kengakuin research institute?

Kengakuin was a neutral international facility that operated outside the favor or influence of any of the Five Great Nations. Given its official mission of "working toward a world order without interference or profiting from any country," it would be an international scandal if shinobi from the Land of Fire were found to have entered the facility illegally.

That's why we have to do it so no one finds out, Shikamaru said lightly but also with the understanding that he would be the one most criticized if they were discovered trespassing. As an adviser since the time of the Sixth, he bore the greatest burden of risk.

Shikamaru pulled out a chair from a table at the café in the building. He, Ino, and Choji, and one other mission member sat down around the chic table with carved feet.

"Hey? Where are the beans in this organic coffee from? What? Ongakure? Ugh, no. Their coffee's awful. Okay then, this Gyokuro hot tea is fine." Orochimaru clapped the menu closed and thrust it at the server, and then set his elbows on the table and propped his chin up. "So? Calling me all the way out here, this must be quite the serious mission?"

Yes, this mission was a four-person cell of boar, deer, butterfly, and snake.

Ino was nervous and rubbed her bare shoulders in her sleeveless shirt. It was strange to see the criminal who had once planned the downfall of Konoha sitting among her trusted teammates. To be extremely frank—it was hard to make any sense of it!

Feigning ignorance and letting Ino's look of protest wash over him, Shikamaru spread pieces of paper out on the table. One was a map of the city with routes marked on it. The other was a rough sketch of the Kengakuin head office.

"Our mission is to steal the signs to release the seal on 'the star that never strays' deciphered by the institute. I told you on the train that 'the star that never strays' refers to a satellite the Sage of Six Paths launched. The ultra particles hidden inside of it are protected by two seals. One keeps the satellite circling the planet. The other is on the vessel with the ultra particles in it."

"These signs—I thought Sasuke and Sakura brought them back from the astronomical observatory?" Choji cocked his head to one side.

"They did," Shikamaru responded. "Unfortunately, the text is really old, and the place with the second set of signs is smudged and impossible to read. That's why we asked the director of the institute to take a look at it."

"That would be this Furieh who was caught yesterday, right?" Ino said.

Shikamaru nodded. "I made a mistake in giving him *Map of the Heavens*. I knew he wasn't on the up and up. But there was no other person who could restore a text that damaged."

"Oh my! I could have done it," Orochimaru said, looking upset.

Shikamaru stared at him, a complicated look on his face. *I'm not exactly sure you're a* person *though.* He bit back this argument and continued.

"Anyway. Furieh must have repaired the damage to the ancient text and deciphered it. Otherwise, he couldn't have released the seal on the vessel and gotten the ultra particles out. He must have gotten the signs for both 'the sky that fell to the earth' and 'the star that never strays,' but he still hasn't regained consciousness. And without his testimony, Kengakuin won't admit to the scandal. But we don't have time to argue with them."

"So we're just going to go in and hack the man's computer," Ino said.

"Right," Shikamaru replied. "The text is who knows how many hundreds of years old. There's no way he was sitting there with a magnifying glass, poring over it. The work had to have been done on a computer. Orochimaru, that's why I asked you along."

"I understand. But don't forget about my compensation, hm?"

This compensation Orochimaru insisted on was the blue-print for the system bike Chihare had developed. He apparently wanted to make and ride one of his own.

Shikamaru nodded reluctantly. "I haven't." He shifted his gaze to Choji and Ino. "The institute firewall won't let anyone in unless they're at a terminal with access authorization. On top of that, Furieh's computer has its own individual security. So from here on out, we split into two groups."

He set a photo down on top of the map. It was of a young man in an expensive-looking suit.

"This guy's the head of the Technology Department, Chomen Nohto. He's the one with firewall authorization. Choji and I will approach him and get it unlocked one way or another."

"So then..." Ino guessed at her team assignment and gulped as she turned her eyes toward Orochimaru.

"Ino, you pair up with Orochimaru and break into the institute," Shikamaru continued. "Once we take down the firewall, you hack Furieh's computer and get the deciphered sign data."

Seeing Ino's face tense up, Orochimaru smiled, pleased. "Looking forward to it. ♡"

"We've got until ten p.m. That's when Naruto and the others will reach the satellite."

"Hey, so what if we don't make it in time?" Choji asked. "What if the vessel isn't open when Naruto and them get to it?"

"Sasuke'll smash it," Shikamaru replied easily. "The vessel's protected by powerful wards, but there's nothing that guy can't smash."

"So then we don't really need to do all this sneaking around?" Ino said, and Shikamaru was at a loss for words. He glanced at Orochimaru.

"It's a natural question." Orochimaru pulled his head back and continued coolly. "The substance inside the vessel amplifies chakra. If a shinobi like Sasuke, with a vast amount of chakra, were to be showered in it, their chakra vessels would explode and they would die instantly."

"What... that," Ino stammered. "Does Sasuke..."

"He knows." Shikamaru scratched his head, annoyed. "Still, he'll happily smash it for Naruto's sake. He's that kind of guy."

"But if Sasuke does that, then Sakura and Sarada..." Ino protested.

"He honestly believes that everyone will be fine as long as Naruto's around," Shikamaru told her. "He seriously doesn't get that just like how his family is important to him, he's also important to his family."

"He's a real idiot," Choji said gently, and Shikamaru nodded his head in agreement.

"Well, it's a hassle, but... This mission's not just to save Naruto. Sasuke's life is also on the line here."

"We can't mess this one up, huh?" Ino said finally.

The three of them exchanged powerful looks. It had been a long time since all three members of the Ino-Shika-Cho team had come together. On top of that, their mission objective involved Naruto and Sasuke, which ignited a bigger fire in their hearts.

"I apologize for intruding on your passionate little moment," Orochimaru interjected, bringing his teacup and saucer up in front of his chest. "But in order to release the seal on the vessel in the satellite, won't you have to go all the way to the Land of Redaku and weave the signs there? In the text, it says you 'must tarry in the Land of Redaku reveling with the Map of the Heavens.' What if this 'reveling with the Map of the Heavens' is alluding to weaving the signs hidden in the book?"

"Yeah, it won't work unless the signs are woven in the Land of Redaku," Shikamaru agreed. "We got someone headed that way now."

For a man who generally did not let his feelings show, Orochimaru looked perplexed.

This strategy had been decided on the previous night. Even if this "someone" had set off for Redaku at the very moment the decision was made, no one could reach the Land of Redaku—

"He exists. We've got the perfect person for this job." Ino smiled proudly. "Someone who can fly faster than anyone, and who'll definitely be able to receive my Mind Transmission."

The bird spread its black-ink wings and flew.

The fastest flying creature in Sai's Cartoon Beast Mimicry was the yadonaki goose, a legendary water bird that passed over mountains and rivers with such grace and elegance that it was said to have caused envy in travelers walking along the ground. Its long fluttering tail feathers were particularly beautiful, and its flying figure, supple like that of an angel, had charmed many a painter.

Sai was currently working this vision of a bird like a carriage horse.

"Keee…" The yadonaki let out a short cry and turned its long neck reproachfully toward Sai. It probably wanted a break, but Sai shook his head, his face expressionless, and stroked its inky feathers consolingly.

Built for speed, the yadonaki was meant for carrying letters and packages; it certainly wasn't intended to carry people. The bird struggled to keep flying with its creator Sai on its back. He must have weighed so heavily on the poor creature.

I'm pushing it too hard, he thought. But this mission required movement in a mere twenty hours across a distance that would take twenty days on shinobi feet and two days at the speed of a hawk. If he didn't push, he wouldn't make it in time.

Honestly, I'm a terrible boss.

Sai wiped away the sweat beading on his forehead. If the yadonaki was pushing and straining itself, its creator Sai was also pushing and straining himself.

When Shikamaru came to the Anbu office the previous night, he said he'd explain everything later and shoved a map into Sai's hand. *Get to this place before ten p.m. tomorrow night,* he said. And the map was just a direction and a distance scribbled onto a piece of straw paper.

This distance by ten tomorrow?

This was a bit much, even for an urgent mission. He got the details of the situation while he prepared for the trip. He was surprised to learn that Naruto was seriously ill, and he was also angry that Shikamaru had hidden this from him. But before he had the chance to complain about it, Shikamaru was practically kicking him out the door and on his way. He'd been flying without sleep or a break ever since, with nothing but his compass for guidance.

Even with the yadonaki's flying abilities, it was a gamble whether he'd make it within the specified time. And then when he got there, he had to receive a message from his wife using Mind Transmission and weave some signs. He'd gotten messages from her via Mind Transmission before, things like, "Please stop by the store on your way home," but this was the first time they'd have such a great distance between them.

Haah. Sai exhaled a shallow breath.

It was harder to breathe because they'd gained altitude so rapidly.

They'd long since passed the countries within his familiar cultural sphere, and there was nothing but desolate mountains below them now.

"It's really there, right? An actual country with people in a place like this…"

Naruto couldn't relax. He looked over the proposal before his eyes for the hundredth time. "The cost of equipment accompanying the adoption of the new curriculum of kunai throwing increased five hundred thousand ryo over last year," "adoption of a preferential selection system for the classics lesson and separate collection for teaching material costs"—Shino had apparently poured her heart into this academy budget proposal for the next fiscal year, but the words scattered in all directions on the page when Naruto set his eyes on them.

Aah, this is pointless. I'm not getting anything from this.

The hands of the clock showed five thirty. Sakura was supposed to come pick him up from the house at eight.

"I'm heading out!" He leaped to his feet. He hadn't met his quota for the day, but he could make it all up with however much overtime was necessary tomorrow once all of this was taken care of.

There was no one home when he got there. He belatedly recalled Hinata saying something about taking Himawari over to say hi to her father.

Naruto wandered around the empty house. It was all fine and good to have come home, but he still couldn't relax. It had been ages since he'd even been in the house at this hour on a weekday. He had no idea what to do with himself; he had way too much time on his hands. With no other ideas, he sat down on the sofa and was staring through the TV when Boruto came home.

"Dad." Boruto's eyes grew wide when he popped his head into the living room. "You're early today, huh?"

"Yeah. Well," Naruto said. "But sorry, I can't train with you today."

"It's fine. No big," Boruto said curtly and ran up the stairs to his own room.

He seems weird somehow. Is he actually angry I can't train with him? Or did something happen on a mission?

His thoughts whirled around in his head. It was hard to figure out his son's feelings.

"Okay, so!" For some reason, Boruto was back in the living room.

"Huh? Problem? What's up?" Naruto craned his neck back.

"Okay! Listen!" Boruto stamped his feet in frustration. "I know I said all that stuff to you before about you being home more... But I don't care about that anymore! And I'll take care of Mom and Himawari. I'm gonna work real hard, so you can just work hard for the village, Dad."

Ohh. Naruto finally got it.

Boruto was worried that it was his fault that Naruto had been coming home earlier lately. He was apparently embarrassed to be saying all of this to Naruto because the tip of his small nose was colored the slightest bit red.

"You're a good kid." Naruto let the words that popped into his head slip out of his mouth, and Boruto turned completely red.

"I'm not good or whatever!" he half-yelled, kicked Naruto's shin, and then stomped away to his own room.

Listening to the loud footfalls, Naruto started laughing. "That kid... Always gotta take the hard way."

Eight p.m.

As promised, Sakura pulled up in front of the Uzumaki house on the system bike.

Boruto was surprised by the sound of the engine and ran outside to see what was going on. His eyes flew open when he saw the bike. "Whoa! You're riding some serious mecha, Sarada's mom! So cool!"

"It's called a bike, a vehicle for individual mobility," Sakura told him. "You don't have to check the schedule and head to the station like when you take the train. You can just go whenever you want."

"Wow. Does it shoot lasers?" Boruto asked, eyes glittering.

"Hmm. There might be a model like that in the future," Sakura replied noncommittally.

"I definitely want to take a ride on that!" Boruto cried. "I'll get Mitsuki or Shikadai or someone on the back and race around the village!"

"It's not safe riding around the village," Naruto retorted as he stepped out of the house. The fact that he'd raced through the alleys and lanes of the village with Chihare riding behind him was a secret. "Where's everyone else?"

"Sasuke went on ahead to the training ground. Master Kakashi and Commander Yamato might be a little late," Sakura said. "I guess they were up all night practicing. Said they used all their chakra and their energy, so they were dead asleep until just a little bit ago."

"Yeah?"

Sakura noticed Naruto's face stiffen slightly and smiled. "What? You nervous?"

"Of course not!" Naruto denied the charge overenthusiastically, yanked the goggles he had around his neck up above his forehead, and straddled the bike behind Sakura.

Chihare had been gradually making improvements to her design, and now there was a speedometer and a brake lever that hadn't been on the prototype. The biggest change was the conversion device added to the engine. Chakra in the cartridge was changed into Kizahashi gas to supply fuel to the tank, dramatically increasing the mileage. It could now go about two thousand kilometers on one fully charged cartridge.

"It's got brakes now, huh?" Naruto noted.

"Yup. But it can't stop suddenly. You have to slow down and then come to a stop." Sakura put a foot on the pedal and pulled the lever.

Vrrr!

The engine roared to life, and the bike pulled forward in a stable movement. Thanks to the tweaks Chihare had made, it was much more pleasant to ride than it had been on his last trip.

"Dad's so lucky..." Boruto watched them go, enraptured.

The bike arrived at the training ground in no time flat. Sasuke wasn't the only one there—Kakashi and Yamato had also arrived, but they looked sleepy, like they had just woken up. They were putting their backs together, pulling on each other's arms, doing stretches.

"I need to hook you up to some supplemental oxygen," Sakura said. "Naruto, Sasuke, show me your stomachs."

Both men did as they were told and lifted their shirts. Sakura inserted an IV needle into the chakra channel next to Sasuke's bellybutton, and followed it with one in a vein on his side.

The needles were connected through the pluripotent applicator hanging from his belt. It would change the chakra collected from the channel into oxygen and supply that directly to his bloodstream.

Since Naruto couldn't supply chakra himself, she connected him to Sasuke's chakra channel as well.

This was the ultra-compact oxygen supply device that Chihare had stayed up all night making.

"No matter what, the two of you make sure to stay together. If the tube comes out, Naruto will lose his oxygen supply."

Sakura painted quick-drying cement on the base of the needles to fix them in place. Now they'd be able to breathe even two hundred kilometers up in the air. In theory.

The tube connecting the oxygen device on Sasuke to Naruto's vein was about two and a half feet long. Naruto felt the ground shift under his feet a bit when he thought about how his life now depended on this long, skinny thing. He stared down at the needle stabbed into his side.

Gotta make sure to stay right close to Sasuke...

"Let's go over everything one more time now that we're all here," Yamato called out to the others, having finished his warm-up exercises.

"The plan is for me and Kakashi to create a pillar of wood and earth. You three run the bike up that pillar. If you go at exactly 125 miles an hour, the point you reach in an hour will be 660,000 feet in the air. If you're going to knock the satellite out of the sky at just the right moment, you must maintain that pace. You can't go too fast or too slow."

"We prioritized strength when we worked this technique out, so while I can't say it'll be a smooth ride up the surface of the pillar, do the best you can with it, okay?" Kakashi said.

Sakura nodded. "Okay."

"So once the satellite approaches, get Naruto to use the Byakugan and get close to it. There's a seal on the ultra particles' vessel inside, but Team Ino-Shika-Cho and Sai are going to take care of that for us, so it should be unlocked by the time you reach the satellite. Handle the details as they come," Kakashi said lightly.

"Same thing as always," Sakura said. No matter how many simulations they ran, they couldn't predict exactly what might happen. Everyone was used to adapting and reacting in the moment.

At last, it was time.

The three shinobi got on the bike. In the lead, hands on the grips, was Sakura in charge of chakra control. Naruto rode behind her, assisting with their approach to the satellite with the power of his goggles, and Sasuke sat behind him to supply chakra to the engine.

The system bike had been conceived as a two-passenger vehicle, so it was a tight squeeze with the three of them on the seat. Wedged in between the married Uchihas, Naruto tried to make himself smaller.

"Eight fifty-nine. One minute." Sakura looked at the pocket watch and counted down.

Mission start was nine sharp.

"Three...two...one..."

Instead of saying "zero," Sakura tossed the pocket watch.

Yamato and Kakashi exchanged a look and slapped the palms of their hands against the earth.

"Earth Style!"

"Wood Style!"

"Rasenro!" they shouted together.

Zwwm!

Pillars of earth and wood shot up toward the sky, intertwining and alternating with each other. With no time to be awed by the beautiful helix, Sakura kicked hard at the pedal of the system bike.

Vrrr!

The vehicle bucked at the sudden acceleration and, with three people on its seat, raced vertically up the Rasenro pillar.

Chapter 5

Eight p.m.

Shikamaru and Choji showed their fake IDs at the entrance and marched up the dim staircase of a certain nightclub in the shopping district.

The place was booming, despite its being a weekday, and most of the lockers were in use. On the atrium of the dance floor, men and women were jumbled together, moving their bodies to the explosively loud house music.

Shikamaru and Choji got drinks at the bar, then found a place near the wall to scout out their target. According to their intel, Chomen Nohto was the rare scientist who loved going out at night, the party animal type. It had taken them longer than they'd expected to pinpoint the location of this club, his recent favorite which he frequented every night. Fortunately, however, they soon spotted Nohto.

"There," Choji said to Shikamaru, hiding his mouth behind his glass of beer. "Sofa seat. Three men, three women. Six-person group."

Shikamaru casually turned his eyes toward the sofa seating

that looked down over the atrium. Nohto was toasting the others at his table with a shot glass of distilled liquor.

"The men he's with are shinobi, hm?" he said. "Glasses and Long Hair. Maybe bodyguards."

"And bait for talking to women," Choji added. "Just being a shinobi in the Land of Kizahashi is enough to get all the dates you want."

The pair watched Nohto for a bit. The three women left the table and went down to the dance floor, while the men kept drinking at a hard pace.

"Pouring drinks down their throats like that, he'll be headed for the washroom soon," Choji noted.

"Right?" Shikamaru agreed. "Let's get him then."

But contrary to their expectations, Nohto didn't get up. The other two men went to the washroom in turn, but Nohto remained sunk into the sofa, polishing off one drink after another, orange peels and all.

Just when Shikamaru had started to think that they would have to try a different tactic, Nohto finally stood up and headed for the washroom.

At last.

Shikamaru and Choji signaled each other with their eyes, moved toward the washrooms, and waited for Nohto to come out.

A minute or so later.

"Hey! It's been ages!" Shikamaru called out amiably to Nohto and threw an arm over his shoulders.

"Huh?" Nohto frowned suspiciously.

Shikamaru kept moving his arm up around Nohto's neck and pulled it tighter. Nohto wheezed for breath and in less than seven seconds, he was completely unconscious.

"Aah. What? I told you you drink too much." Propping Nohto up, Shikamaru made like he was taking care of a friend who'd had a bit too much and dragged him back into the men's washroom.

Luckily, there was no one else in the large room. With purple lights illuminating the tiled floor and walls, the interior design was really something.

Shikamaru pushed Nohto into the stall furthest back and frisked him. He found a portable terminal about the size of a business card case in one pocket.

"This it?"

He touched the screen, and four blank squares popped up, together with the words "Please enter your passcode." Apparently, the machine used an electrostatic touchscreen.

He took a small bag from his pocket and sprinkled the adhesive powder inside on the screen. The powder would stick to the oil from Nohto's fingers on the touchscreen and highlight his fingerprints, which would be concentrated in the places he touched most frequently.

The numbers with the most powder covering them were 8, 1, and 0.

"Tch!" Shikamaru unconsciously clicked his tongue.

The passcode was four digits, but he had only three numbers. Which most likely meant the passcode used the same number twice. If they had all been different numbers, then the number of possible combinations was twenty-four, but if one of the numbers was a double, that increased to thirty-six combinations.

At any rate, all he could do was start from one end and try them all. Shikamaru hurriedly tapped at the screen.

8810, 8801, 8108, 8018, 8081, 8180—

"Nohto? Are you okay?"

He'd tried about ten combinations when he heard a voice from the entrance.

Concerned about Nohto's long absence, his companions— Glasses and Long Hair—had come looking for him.

Shikamaru and Choji reflexively held their breath, but no matter how quiet they were, only one of the stall doors was closed, and six feet could be seen below it. There was no way that wasn't going to arouse suspicion.

Shikamaru decided to lure the two men in and deliberately made a sound as he slid the lock open. He knocked lightly on the inside of the door and waited.

The men came to stand in front of the stall.

"Nohto? Are you in there?"

Choji brandished a fist and launched a full-powered punch straight at Glasses' stomach as he threw open the door.

While Shikamaru and Choji were examining Nohto's body in the narrow men's washroom stall, Ino and Orochimaru had transformed themselves into researchers and were boldly walking into the Kengakuin head office.

Ino had changed her face to look like a middle-aged scientist at least, but Orochimaru was wearing his usual face. Ino had no idea if it was his true face though, nor did she want to find out.

I cannot believe I'm here walking with the *Orochimaru.*

She glanced at the snake man beside her and shrugged to herself. Mass murder, terrorism, developing forbidden jutsu, human experimentation, theft, kidnapping—Orochimaru's priors were a hit parade of the most serious crimes. To think that she was buddied up with a man like this. She half-expected him to kill her on a whim in the middle of the mission.

"I wonder what floor the office is on," he said abruptly, and Ino nearly jumped out of her skin.

"Oh. R-r-right. I wonder what floor'd be good."

"Hm?" He turned doubtful yellow eyes on her.

Yikes! That sounded weird, she thought in a panic as the elevator arrived.

"The director's office is, let's see, the thirteenth floor!" She checked the display on the elevator panel and then jammed her hand against the buttons. She'd meant to push thirteen but hit eight accidentally. Orochimaru's gaze grew more and more doubtful.

Ino shrank into herself. She missed her usual team.

The bike carrying Sakura, Naruto, and Sasuke raced up the wall of wood and earth, engine roaring.

It had been about five minutes since they started out. At some point, they'd passed through a thin cloud, and the ground had long ago disappeared from sight. If they were on target, they were just shy of 55,000 feet up. The wind grew so strong that keeping their eyes open was painful, but the bike itself was plastered to the pillar with chakra control and didn't so much as twitch.

"Good thing the stars are out," Sakura said, mostly to herself, her hands on the grips. The bike didn't have a light of any kind, but thanks to the bright stars, she could clearly see the path of the pillar. But just as she uttered that, the area abruptly grew darker.

"Hm?" Suddenly, droplets of water were spraying her face.

"Pwah! Cold!" Naruto yelped.

"Looks like we've entered a cloud," Sasuke remarked.

The tiny drops of water beat at their bodies from all directions like scattershot, and in no time at all, the three of them were drenched. Each drop was a tiny bit of mist on its own, but the speed they were moving made them sting. Worse yet, as they rode further into the cloud, the droplets changed into pellets of ice. Now they really hurt.

"Cumulonimbus cloud maybe," Sakura mused. "There weren't any clouds over the training ground, so it must have drifted in from somewhere."

"This is bad! Believe it! If it rains down there, Master Kakashi and Commander Yamato will—"

A dazzling light flashed inside of the cloud and quickly disappeared. Static electricity began to crackle around Sasuke's and Sakura's hair. The cumulonimbus cloud appeared to be developing into a thunder cloud.

A cold sweat popped up on Sakura's already wet forehead. "This is maybe not the time for us to be worried about the masters down below."

Ba ba boom!

They heard an ear-splitting roar, and then the area was enveloped in a pure white light before a bolt of lightning hit the bike. Naruto and Sasuke immediately flew up off the seat, but in different directions. They shot past each other, jerking the oxygen tube taut.

"Whoa!" Naruto grabbed Sasuke's shoulder and pulled his friend toward himself as he tossed a kunai into the Rasenro to create a foothold that just barely held the two of them. His face grew pale. "Where's Sakura?!"

She had dropped down with the bike after it was knocked flying by the lightning.

"It's fine. She'll come up soon enough," Sasuke said evenly and turned his gaze downward.

Vrrr!

The bike and Sakura raced up the pillar. She picked up Sasuke and Naruto as she passed by and charged upward once more.

"Sakura! You're okay!" Naruto said in relief. "I was freaked that you maybe fell down."

"I can handle a little something like that," she replied, while next to her ear, her hair burned with a *crack*. Sparks of static electricity bounced around her head. "Looks like another hit's coming. *We* might be fine, but I don't know how much this bike can take."

The cloud lit up once more, and the air crackled. It was only a matter of time before they were struck by lightning again.

"I'll cut it." Sasuke put a foot on the wheel and stood up.

"What?!" Sakura cried, in surprise. "You can *do* that?"

"Did you forget the other name for Chidori?" Sasuke replied and kneaded his chakra in his hand. He produced a lump of earth, and in the blink of an eye, he'd sharpened its outlines to form a kunai. *Ting!* The earth turned into glass. He'd applied an Earth Style technique to change the ratio of elements included in the earth to fashion an impromptu kunai.

The hand that clutched the glass kunai began to make a chirping sound and sing with electricity.

As if taking the bait, the cloud was blanketed in white light, and lightning struck the bike once more.

Crack crack crack!

It was too loud and bright, and Sakura didn't know what was going on. When the echoes of the thunder faded from her eardrums at last, drawing out a long tail, she looked back and saw Sasuke with his foot on the wheel like nothing had happened.

"You cut it?" she asked, stunned, as she blinked eyes dazzled by the light.

Perhaps temporarily deafened by the roar, Sasuke didn't respond, so Naruto answered on his behalf, "He cut it."

Thanks to the Byakugan, he'd seen everything. A few seconds before the discharge, Sasuke tossed the kunai, and the tip of it severed the lightning bolt. Exposed to that incredible electrical heat, the kunai was instantly destroyed, but the glass, with its insulating properties, had indeed cut through the lightning. The bolt was ripped in two, and these remnants were lured away by Sasuke's Chidori, one forcibly pulled toward the sky, the other toward the ground, before they vanished entirely.

Naruto smelled burning. He glanced back and saw that Sasuke's hair and cloak were singed.

Whoa, he really did that, Naruto said in his heart, duly impressed.

Sasuke's Chidori had truly cut lightning.

Naruto, Sasuke, and Sakura weren't the only ones fighting without their feet on the ground.

Sai, a member of Team Seven, was also dashing through the sky. Although unlike Naruto and the others who were moving vertically, Sai's movement was horizontal.

He had been ascending steadily since he approached the mountains, so that he was now at an altitude of nearly 16,500 feet.

"Are we still not there..." Sai flopped forward against the yadonaki goose.

Headache, trouble breathing, extreme fatigue. All symptoms of altitude sickness. Without an oxygen tube like Naruto and his team had, Sai was, to be blunt, in a living hell.

No matter how strong he might have been as a shinobi, he still couldn't live without oxygen. In contrast with Sakura, Kakashi, and even Sasuke, who had chosen routes without dramatic altitude increases to allow their bodies to adjust as they made their way to the Land of Redaku, Sai had ascended to that same altitude in mere hours.

"Haah... Hah! Koff! Haah..." He couldn't breathe. Pain rocked his head from the inside, dulling his thinking.

The Land of Redaku...is too far...

After two hours spent looking dejectedly out over the mountains, a town made by human hands appeared at last in a small plain surrounded by exposed rock, and his cold sweat stopped.

"There it is..."

The yadonaki began to glide down toward the settlement.

The men's washroom was in chaos.

The man in glasses who had opened the stall door dug deep inside to brace himself while he took a punch to the gut and then threw a daring knee into Choji's side as the shinobi tried to slip past. Behind him, Shikamaru was wedged between Choji as he came flying back and the toilet pipes and cut his ear and cheek. But Nohto behind him had even worse luck and cracked his head against the porcelain toilet while still unconscious.

It was a free for all.

"These guys are tough! What's going on?!" Glasses yelled.

But Long Hair was tangling with Shikamaru and didn't have time for chitchat. They tumbled around on the floor, each stealing the top spot from the other over and over.

Glasses desperately grabbed Choji's collar. He yanked it forward, but Choji's core was too strong and he didn't budge. Choji grabbed Glasses' necktie and slammed him into the wall. As Glasses collapsed along with part of the wall, Choji charged to finish him off, but Glasses nimbly spun around and used that force and momentum to pull the pipe out of the toilet.

A surge of water clobbered Choji, fixing him in place momentarily.

He felt a prickling pain race up his fleshy back.

"Huh?" He reached around and felt a small needle. His body grew numb, and he dropped to his knees. He looked back and saw that the man with long hair had the barrel of a gun turned toward him, even while Shikamaru sat on top of him pummeling him with blows.

"What did you do?!" Shikamaru grabbed the back of Long Hair's head and pressed it into the flood on the floor.

Needle. Poison?

"Choji! You okay?!" he called.

"Fine." Choji had already finished weaving the signs by the time he replied in a low voice.

Multi-Size Technique!

His body abruptly swelled and expanded outward. With the washroom very much unable to contain his rapidly growing bulk, Choji smashed the walls and pushed up against the ceiling.

The lethal dose of a poison depended on the size of the body. If the body were enormous, then the required lethal dose would also need to increase. If he made himself a little taller, if he grew to about sixteen feet, then one shot of poison would no longer have any effect on him.

"What the..."

Glasses and Long Hair gaped, and by the time they came back to themselves, Shikamaru was gone. While Choji was tearing the washroom apart, Shikamaru had flown the coop.

"Haah! It's cold," Naruto sighed, as they finally broke through the top of the cloud. How many times had he witnessed Sasuke's superhuman art of cutting lightning after that first strike?

The air around them was below freezing, and they were all covered in ice pellets. Naruto brushed away the ice that clung to Sakura's neck and shoulders, and Sasuke brushed away the ice building up on Naruto's head. Since no one could do the same for Sasuke at the end of the line, he shook himself like a cat drenched in the rain and knocked the ice off himself.

The area was calm like they'd flown onto an atoll, making their terrible journey through the cloud seem like an impossibility. Space lay ahead of the extending pillar, and the stars shone like gold dust in the riverbed of the starry sky, clear like a small brook. The light reflecting off the startlingly large moon was so sharp, it seemed like he could almost grab hold of it, but unfortunately, the threesome didn't have the luxury of enjoying the view.

"Honestly. That was no fun at all," Sakura said wearily and looked down. A cloud hung far below, looking like a goat's back.

It was definitely a cumulonimbus cloud. There was a real possibility it was raining on the ground. "I hope the masters are okay."

Sakura's hope was not borne out—the village of Konohagakure was being assaulted by a downpour.

"Ah, this isn't good," Kakashi had said when a drop of rain hit his nose a mere two minutes earlier.

The downpour began in earnest almost instantly, raining down without mercy. Both earth and wood grew softer from the wetness. The earth pillar was particularly susceptible to moisture, and the surface quickly began to crumble. He would have to use extra chakra to reinforce it and keep it from falling over.

"If we keep using chakra at this pace, we definitely won't make it to 660,000 feet!" Yamato cried. "Kakashi, what should we do?"

"What should we do?" Kakashi muttered, his hands still planted on the ground. "I guess all we can do is keep trying."

The elevator deposited Ino and Orochimaru on the thirteenth floor with a little mechanical hum. The director's office should have been at the end of a long hallway, but they had only taken a few steps when a thick, steel door blocked the way ahead. The security system to one side clearly used fingerprint and optical authentication for entry. If an unregistered person attempted to get in, an alarm would no doubt sound.

"So a card's too old school then," Ino sighed.

"I could destroy it all?" Orochimaru said evenly.

Ino shook her head dejectedly. Ino-Shika-Cho missions were centered around intelligence gathering, for the most part. The rule was they left no trace of themselves behind. And now this snake man comes along, ready to burn it all down.

"So don't break it? Then I'll at least hack into the security cameras." A snake slithered out from the hem of Orochimaru's kimono. It wriggled up the wall and wrapped itself around the camera hanging from the ceiling, bit into it, made a hole in the side, stuck its slender tongue in, and began flicking it around.

Ino and Orochimaru had likely already been filmed standing in front of the door, which meant that if they stayed there, someone would come along eventually. They could continue to play the researchers and eloquently plead their case and get them to open it, or...

While Ino's thoughts raced, a voice came from behind them.

"You two. What are you doing there?"

When Ino looked back, a woman in a grey suit was walking toward them. She had to have seen the snake wrapped around the security camera, but perhaps Orochimaru had cast a genjutsu on her—she paid it no mind as she marched straight toward them.

"This floor is off limits to anyone without permission."

"Oh! Umm. We needed to speak with Director Furieh." Ino played the timid scientist and shrank into herself as she replied. "Um. Who are you?"

"Mr. Furieh's secretary," the woman replied, puffing her chest out.

His secretary would definitely be able to get through the security to the director's office. On a normal mission, Ino wouldn't have hesitated to borrow the woman's body with Mind Transmission. But while she was using the jutsu, her body was completely defenseless, so she only used it when she was with trusted comrades. Was Orochimaru really the sort of person she could entrust herself to like that?

"Um, we're with the Mathematics Department." Ino pointed to the badge on her chest. "The equation we discovered seems like it could be applied to the chakra pluripotent applicator research Director Furieh's been moving ahead with. We wanted to discuss it with him."

Hearing the words "pluripotent applicator research," the secretary's expression changed slightly. Furieh had Chihare working on that project in secret, and only a few people in the institute knew anything about it.

She stared hard at Ino and Orochimaru. "Which section do you belong to?"

"The mathematical analysis team." They chorused the answer they'd prepared at the strategy meeting earlier.

"And the project?"

"Representation of degenerate principal series and Simple Lie group representation methods," they said in unison.

The secretary thought for a moment. "Show me evidence of your research."

"What? We don't walk around with that." Ino shrugged exaggeratedly. "We left it on our desks."

"But we can share the details of our research and prove that we're scholars," Orochimaru said and then began to explain at top speed. "In the development of a technology applying frequency analysis discretized further with digital signals for the conventional transformation to convert the real variable of a real-valued function to a similar type of function, we created a formula to carry out frequency analysis for the interval signal— which is to say, n multiplied by a complex number. This expresses the mapping onto the complex function, and while this does utilize unitary operator theory, when carrying out calculations with practical values, summing up the normalization factors into one, at the point when we simultaneously scale up—"

"Fine, yes, okay, I understand," the secretary cut Orochimaru off, seemingly fed up. "Happily lecturing about your personal theories with zero regard for time and place, you're definitely one of our researchers. I'll give you that.

But you can't see Mr. Furieh. He hasn't returned since yesterday."

"Since yesterday?" Although she knew this, Ino kept any hint of that off her face and made a show of widening her eyes in surprise. "That's worrying. Was he in an accident or something?"

"He often gets absorbed in his research, so it's not particularly unusual," the secretary said, unconcerned.

Ino glanced up at the security camera. The snake was curled up on top of it. It was done hacking it.

"I'll have to ask you to please leave." The secretary put a haughty hand on her hip. "I know that none of our scientists have actually taken a good look at the company rules, but at the very least, you should know you can't go any further than this without permission. You have to follow proper procedures and come again."

This wasn't going to end peacefully. In which case it seemed that she had no choice but to use Mind Transmission, although she was still uneasy about trusting Orochimaru.

"All right, we'll come again." Ino acted like they would obediently withdraw and turned her back to the secretary to whisper to Orochimaru. "Distract the secretary? I'll take over her body with Mind Transmission."

"Hm? Oh, that's far too much of a hassle," Orochimaru said and lifted the sleeve of his kimono.

Multiple Striking Shadow Snakes Technique!

A massive albino rat snake flew out from the kimono and wrapped itself around the secretary's body. The armful of torso was hoisted up, and the secretary passed out without the first clue that something was afoot.

It was over in an instant. Ino hadn't even had time to stop him.

"You didn't kill her, right?!" She grabbed Orochimaru by the collar and snapped at him so forcefully she was practically biting him.

"Who can say?" He cocked his head curiously to one side. "Why don't you check yourself?"

Nine thirty-five p.m.

After arriving at the small settlement in the mountains, Sai used the Art of Transformation to match his clothing to the local style and casually strolled around the town.

In front of a longhouse made of sun-dried brick, children were splashing each other over a barrel of water. Skinned wild birds were boiling in full pots in the communal cooking area. And in the center of the slightly elevated rocky mountain, a palace of stone had been built looking out over the town.

The look of the place matched up with what Shikamaru had told him before he came. This was almost certainly the Land of Redaku. Now that he was in the country, all he had to do was wait for the message from Ino and weave the signs.

Redaku's culture seemed fairly different from that of the Five Great Nations, in the style of buildings and the style of clothing, but unfortunately, Sai couldn't enjoy the local color, suffering from altitude sickness as he was.

"Haah... Haah..." When his limbs went numb, he got the feeling he was in serious trouble.

This is bad.

Blearily, Sai stopped himself from clicking his tongue. Would he even be able to weave the signs in this state?

The rain falling on the village of Konohagakure grew stronger with each passing second. Kakashi and Yamato were thoroughly soaked as they poured all of their chakra into the Rasenro.

"Ngh... Haah, this is rough..."

"Hah... Haah!"

They had no sooner reinforced their respective pillars with chakra when the rain sweeping in from the side beat against the Rasenro, soaking it from the inside. There was no end to their struggle. They had to keep it strong enough to hold up against the rain, and the speed at which it grew had dropped significantly.

"Hah! We're in trouble here," Kakashi muttered, looking up. The clouds hung thick in the night sky, and it didn't look like the downpour would be stopping anytime soon. "Our speed is... Hah! Dropping... Like this..."

They wouldn't make it. Not only that, he was starting to doubt how long they could even keep it from falling over.

Kakashi and Yamato had both long since passed their limits. Veins twitched up to the surface of their hands pressed against the ground, their shoulders, temples, and necks, and steam rose up from their overheated bodies. Their gloves had long ago blown off from the pressure of the chakra.

"Ngh!"

"No!"

The earth part of the pillar snapped.

"No... Already?!" Kakashi gave up on extending the pillar and desperately poured his chakra into repairing the rift, but there were limits to the amount of chakra he could release at one time. Soaked to its core, the earthen pillar was crumbling from the inside. On top of that, now that the wooden pillar had lost its partner and support, the extra burden caused cracks in the wood.

No, no, no. It's going to break!

Crack!

Bark tore off of the tree, the trunk split, and the entire structure listed heavily to one side. To prevent its collapse, the two shinobi pushed their chakra into the structure, and the blood vessels popping up on the muscles in their arms jumped about. As if taunting them, the rain grew even stronger, and a violent wind swept toward the pillar.

The creaking, listing Rasenro was going to tumble over.

And then two pairs of arms wedged their way in between Kakashi and Yamato. And then there were four hands slapped against the ground.

Naruto, Sasuke, and Sakura in the sky above noticed a change in the Rasenro.

"The pillar's gradually slowing down, isn't it?" Sakura said, frowning.

"Maybe something happened below?" Sasuke replied.

"Aaah!" Naruto cried out after pulling the lever on the goggles and looking over his shoulder. "It's raining."

"I *knew* it. So that's why the pillar's slowing down." Sakura worked the clutch to fine tune the bike's speed. "They're using up their chakra to keep the pillar strong enough to handle the rain."

"At this pace, we won't make it to 660,000 feet before time runs out," Sasuke noted.

"No, we'll be okay," Naruto said to the Uchiha couple in front of and behind him. "Master Kakashi and Commander Yamato said they would handle it! I'm sure those two can make it work somehow."

"Right." Sakura's expression softened. "They always have, after all. They've overcome impossible situations before. And this mission is pretty rushed, with a lot of moving parts. But I'm sure Master Kakashi and Commander Yamato won't let us down."

Even as they spoke, the speed of the pillar's growth was steadily dropping. Not to mention that the pillar itself had begun to shudder slightly, and its surface was getting brittle and peeling away.

"Actually... This maybe looks not so good." Sakura's gut feeling was timed impeccably—the extension of the pillar at last ceased completely.

The bike couldn't stop suddenly.

"...!"

Sasuke immediately ended the supply of chakra, but the engine didn't stop right away. The bike charged toward the end of the discontinued pillar and shot up into the air.

"Aaaah!"

"Master Kakashiiii?! Commander Yamatoooo?!"

They had two options when the pillar stopped growing. They could go back down with Sasuke's Susano'o, or they could turn around deftly in midair and ride down the pillar. Whichever they chose, the mission was over.

Sakura tightened her hands on the grips and tried turning the bike, while Sasuke started to call Susano'o.

In the next moment, the pillar began to shoot up again.

It grazed the front wheel of the bike, and not missing her chance, Sakura used chakra control to bring together the surfaces of the pillar and the tires.

Bam!

The bike landed heavily on the vertical wall. It wobbled for an instant, but quickly righted itself and started racing upward.

"That was close. I thought it had stopped," Sakura said, wiping away a cold sweat. "But it seems a little different from before?"

Until that moment, pillars of wood and pillars of earth that Yamato and Kakashi were individually responsible for had alternated and twisted around each other as the structure stretched into the sky. But now there were four pillars winding around each other. Three of earth and one of wood. No. There were two earth pillars, and the other one was sand.

"This chakra..." Sasuke said.

Naruto grinned happily. "It's Gaara and Kurotsuchi!"

"Took you long enough."

"Listen, you! You call us the day before the mission, you should be thankful we're even here at all!" Kurotsuchi glared up at Kakashi as she poured chakra into the Rasenro, her hands pressed to the ground. "We just happened to be outside the country on a diplomatic mission, so we could come right away, but... You're about the only person who could just give us a call so easily like this!"

"Naruto's up there?" Gaara said, looking up at the sky with one hand on the ground. "Riding a lump of metal to charge into a cumulonimbus cloud. As reckless as ever, I see."

"Right?" Yamato grinned wryly.

With the assist from Kurotsuchi and Gaara, the Rasenro had regained its strength and was stretching higher into the sky at a stable speed once again.

Yamato's wood pillar, Kakashi's and Kurotsuchi's earth pillars, and Gaara's sand pillar. The four of them wound together like braided hair and rose into the sky, supporting each other as they went. It was a structure more stable than when it had been just the two pillars.

"So why does Naruto want to go 660,000 feet up into the air?" Gaara asked. "There has to be a reason, right?"

"Aaah... I can't tell you that." Even at this late stage, Kakashi was keeping his cards close.

Kurotsuchi looked even more annoyed. "We're here helping you out, and you're not going to tell us the story?"

"Come on, relax. Once this is all over, ask Naruto yourself." Kakashi let her anger glide off him, and Gaara chuckled.

"I suppose we'll do that then," the Kazekage said, sounding like he was having fun, and smiled as he looked up at the growing pillar.

Shikamaru changed his appearance with the Art of Transformation and fled onto the crowded dance floor. He turned on the portable terminal hidden in his coat and entered passcodes one after another.

0018, 0081, 0801, 0108...

"Hey, look there! There's a huge person!"

"For real! He's *massive*!"

The drunk patrons saw the enormous Choji and assumed incorrectly that he was part of some kind of promotion.

Choji had dealt with the poison by expanding, but that meant that he couldn't move for the time being. If he took one wrong step at that size and weight, he'd bring the whole building down.

I'll have to figure this one out on my own.

Shikamaru coolly continued to try passcodes. He'd already run through half of the possibilities, but he still couldn't unlock the device. It was nine forty-five p.m. Finding the club and the unexpected fight with the two men who turned out to be shinobi were unexpected delays. He was out of time. He had to get this firewall down.

Choji turned himself into the mascot of a popular photo-taking spot. Glasses went outside to look for Shikamaru, but Long Hair stayed in the club and was leaning over the railing, scanning the dance floor.

You're fine. Your face and body are different now. Just act naturally, and he won't find you, Shikamaru told himself and kept inputting passcodes.

His performance and his Art of Transformation were indeed perfect. He was even skillfully hiding the unnatural movement of operating the terminal inside of his coat by doing it in time with the flow of people and the beat of the music. If Long Hair had been a normal bodyguard, he would have no doubt decided that the shinobi who assaulted Nohto had fled from the club. But unfortunately, Long Hair was the careful, persistent type.

He got up on a table, pulled a shuriken out of his pocket, and tossed it at the ceiling. The metal carved out a gentle arc in the air, spun around, and stabbed into the fixture attaching the mirror ball to the ceiling.

Snap!

The fixture broke, and the mirror ball dropped toward the packed dance floor.

"That jerk!"

Three women were having the time of their lives in the spot where the mirror ball would land, completely oblivious to their impending doom. Shikamaru grabbed all three of them and lunged forward. The mirror ball hit the floor and shattered, sending tiny pieces of mirror glass in every direction.

"Aaaaah!"

Screams filled the dance floor, and people rushed for the exit.

Shikamaru went against the flow of people, turned his back toward the exit, caught the knee that Long Hair came at him with, and knocked him back with one arm.

"You're the one who stole Nohto's terminal, huh? You're not getting away from me."

Shikamaru feigned innocence. "What are you talking about? I'm just an off-duty ninja who happened to come here to have a little fun."

But Long Hair wasn't having it. He pulled out a sword he had hidden under his jacket.

What a hassle.

Shikamaru inclined the axis of his body and easily dodged Long Hair jumping at him with the sword. While he was at it, he released his transformation jutsu. He feinted like he was going to launch a fist into Long Hair's open side, and then stretched out the shadow at his feet toward Long Hair's shadow as the other man approached almost recklessly.

But a flash of pink light cut across and interrupted his shadow. He tried one more time, but now green and blue lights came one after the other to cut into his shadow. The dance floor of a night club was the worst possible place to use Shadow Possession. The flashing strobe light and the pin lights that wandered across the dance floor kept getting in the way.

Nine forty-seven p.m.

Shikamaru clicked his tongue. *I don't have time to waste with this guy.*

"So this is Furieh's office." Ino looked around the room as she gently set down the secretary in one corner of the room. Given that it was the Kengakuin head honcho's office, she'd assumed it would be fairly luxurious, but there was only a chair and a desk with a computer on it plopped down in the middle of the completely white room.

"She seems heavy. Less of a burden to carry if you'd just taken her eye and her finger," Orochimaru said in a tone that made it impossible for Ino to tell if he was joking or serious, while he tapped away at the computer keyboard.

Ino checked the time on her pocket watch—nine fifty p.m.

Was Shikamaru and Choji's mission going well?

"Orochimaru, how long do you think it'll take you to hack it?" she asked.

"I'm done," he replied immediately.

"What?"

That's too fast?

Surprised, she peered at the monitor, and at the same time, several windows opened. The one at the front read NETWORK PROTECTED in bright red letters.

"I broke through the local security. Now all we can do is wait for those young lads to unlock the firewall."

So that meant that Shikamaru and Choji still hadn't completed their mission.

Ino checked her watch again—nine fifty-one.

Once Shikamaru and Choji unlocked the firewall, Orochimaru would be able to access Furieh's files. Once they got the signs for "the star that never strays" that Furieh deciphered, Ino would send them to Sai in the Land of Redaku with her Mind Transmission. Once Sai wove the signs, the satellite would open, and Naruto and the others would be able to get ahold of the substance inside.

That was their current mission. If any one of them failed, the whole mission would fail.

"Can your jutsu actually reach across such a distance?" Orochimaru asked, as if to fan the flames of her anxiety. "You'll be able to connect all the way to Redaku? To your husband in that far-off land?"

"I've never done it before, so I don't know," she replied honestly, and Orochimaru flicked his tongue out and pulled it back again right away. She continued with a sigh. "During the Great Ninja War, I connected three hundred shinobi all at once. When it comes to connecting three hundred strangers nearby or connecting with one person far away, I feel like the latter's easier. But I've never actually done it, so I can't guarantee it'll go well. But it'll probably be fine."

She was sure of herself. She had no basis for it, but she believed she could do it, because the person she was sending to was the person she knew best in this entire world.

"Hmm. Really," Orochimaru replied disinterestedly, even though he was the one who'd asked about it, and propped his chin up in his hands on the desk.

There was nothing Ino's team could do until Shikamaru's team finished their mission.

Standby.

Intense standby.

Alone with *the* Orochimaru in someone's office.

This is awkward...

Ino opened her pocket watch. Nine fifty-two. She'd had Inojin stay with Sarada at Master Iruka's house starting the previous night. And now tonight, Shikadai and Cho-Cho were there too.

I guess they've already had supper by now, huh?

She glanced down at the whorl on the top of Orochimaru's head as he sat in the chair.

Now that I'm thinking about it, he's Mitsuki's parent. So then does that make us mom friends?

"Mitsuki's a good kid," she said abruptly as she stared at the moving hands of the watch.

"What?" Orochimaru turned himself and the chair around.

"Inojin talks about him a lot. Good grades, always calm. Although I guess he found him hard to hang out with at first. But he says Mitsuki's done some surprisingly stupid stuff with him, and he's a good guy."

"Where did this come from?"

"Nowhere in particular," Ino said. "I figured a parent wants to know about their kid. And you never come to visitors' day and stuff like that, right?"

The narrow, pointed yellow eyes turned toward her. But Orochimaru stopped just short of meeting her gaze, so she wasn't entirely sure if he was really looking at her.

After a brief silence, he said something surprising.

"I went to the parent-teacher interview."

Sai continued to be on standby on the roof of the long house made of sun-dried brick. The sun beating down robbed him of even more strength, and he was already on the verge of dying from lack of oxygen.

He checked the time on the pocket watch he'd brought from the Land of Fire and sighed.

Time was almost up, and he still hadn't gotten a message from Ino.

Nine fifty-eight p.m.

The long hour of driving was over, and the bike and its passengers finally closed in on their targeted distance of 660,000 feet above the ground. The satellite was already entering their field of vision.

With no obstructions around, it stood out clearly, reflecting the light of the sun. The silver sphere appearing, the spinning whirlpools etched onto the sides were reminiscent of the mark of Konoha at first glance.

"We didn't hit the mark after all." Just as Sakura said, the satellite's trajectory was off to the west of the pillar's route by about 165 feet. "I wonder if the ultra particles really are in there."

"Nah, I'm telling you that round thing's a vessel to beat out all vessels. Believe it." Naruto checked it with the Byakugan, and his voice grew darker. "There's a bamboo vessel inside, and it's got the ultra particles in it. But...the wards are still there."

Shikamaru's team hadn't made it in time. The ultra particles were still sealed. At the advance meeting, they'd decided that if the wards hadn't been released at this point in time, they'd abandon the mission and return to the earth.

However.

"Not a problem," Sasuke said curtly and grabbed Naruto.

"Huh?" Baffled, Naruto looked up at Sasuke. Did he have some kind of secret plan? But the look on his face was the same as always.

"Sasuke." Sakura suddenly took her hands off the bike grips and stood up. She twisted her torso around, grabbed Sasuke's collar, and pulled him forcefully toward her. She pressed her lips against his.

"Huh..." Naruto's jaw dropped at the kiss being exchanged above his head.

"I believe in you!" Sakura shouted and then reached into Sasuke's coat, pulled out a headband, and flung it at the approaching satellite.

Naruto very much did not understand what was going on.

This should have been no place for kissing. If they couldn't release the seal in time, they would go back to the ground. That was all. And whose headband was that? Couldn't have been Sasuke's...

Still holding onto Naruto, Sasuke kicked at the wheel and flew up. Having lost its chakra supply, the bike slowed and wobbled, and began to fall with Sakura on it. The headband she had thrown neared the satellite, sparked with the friction of the resistance of what little air still existed at this altitude, and burst into flame before their eyes.

Now charcoal, the headband drifted on the wind and began to crumble.

Ame-no-tejikara!

Sasuke switched himself and Naruto with the decaying charcoal in front of them. The satellite was coming up straight ahead. The air resistance was powerful enough to cause parts of their clothing to spontaneously combust, and Sasuke drew his long sword, pierced the top of his own left foot with the sword's tip, and kept going to stab into the side of the satellite.

Violent, but it got the job done. After fixing the satellite to his own body, Sasuke pulled a sheathed dagger out from his cloak.

"Hang on, Sasuke!" Naruto cried. "The seal on the ultra particles is still there!"

"Not a problem. I'll smash the vessel."

"Idiot! If you do that..." Naruto swallowed the rest of his words, and the color drained from his face. "You're not actually..."

Sasuke didn't answer. The usual expression on his face. He was calm, as if to say that he was simply doing what had to be done.

"You've gotta be kidding me!" Naruto shouted and began to squirm against Sasuke. "Listen to me! You think anyone's gonna be happy if you die to keep me alive?!"

He'd known Sasuke was an idiot, but he hadn't thought he was *this* much of an idiot. Did he think that all the village needed was Naruto? How many thousands of times did he have to tell him, "I need you" and "You're my best friend" and all that before it finally got through to that ridiculously well-formed head?

Sasuke had always been like this, always ready to sacrifice himself. He really believed that if there was a world where everyone except Sasuke was happy and Sasuke alone suffered immensely, then that world was at peace. Just like Sasuke needed Naruto, Naruto needed Sasuke—it was such an obvious thing, and yet no matter how many years passed, no matter what Naruto said, Sasuke didn't get that.

"Are you listening to me?! I'm telling you to let me go!"

"Say sorry to your wife for me," Sasuke said bafflingly, before clamping his teeth down on the sheathe of his dagger and pulling the blade free.

Kashnk!

Shikamaru slammed into the hot pin light with his back. The exposed heated wires touched him, and he heard the sound of sizzling flesh.

Without giving him the time to feel the heat of his wounds, Long Hair charged. Shikamaru leaped to the right to dodge the body blow, and a kunai whizzed past the end of his nose, like it had been lying in wait for him.

"Come *on*!"

Long Hair had been well trained, as one would expect for the bodyguard of a Kengakuin VIP. Shikamaru was forced into a defensive battle while he kept putting in passcodes.

1180.

He still hadn't found the correct passcode for the terminal hidden in his sleeve. This one made thirty-five combinations. The last one left had to be the correct one.

It was almost ten o'clock. Seriously dicey.

Taking advantage of Shikamaru's distraction with the terminal, Long Hair came barreling at him. He grabbed Shikamaru's chin and knocked him to the floor.

Not good, Shikamaru thought, and in the next instant, the palm of an enormous hand swept in from the side and mowed Long Hair down.

"Choji!" Shikamaru lifted his face with a gasp, and Choji pressed on his stomach and fell over. Other than the enormous arm, the rest of him had returned to his original size. The Art of Partial Expansion. "Don't release your expansion technique! The poison will spread, and you'll die!"

"I...know!"

Poof!

In a puff of smoke, Choji's body swelled up again.

Long Hair was splayed out on the floor, not moving.

1108.

When he input the remaining four-digit combination, the lock on the terminal was released. "Yes!"

He tapped on the firewall icon displayed on the screen. A string of characters popped up that would have been totally meaningless to someone who didn't know the rules, a special language only understood by a computer.

Shikamaru deftly input the algorithm for the command "unlock system." After that, all he had to do was tap "execute." But.

"This is such a hassle!"

A bloody fist grazed the top of his head where he was crouched over. The man with the long hair had stubbornly come back to life.

"I got you now!" Long Hair brandished a kunai, blood streaming from his nose and mouth.

Shikamaru kicked him in the stomach and sent him slamming into the wall. The portable terminal hidden inside his coat had returned to the lock screen.

"Ah! Dammit!"

1108. He impatiently input the passcode and found the firewall system fortunately still open, complete with the algorithm Shikamaru had input.

Long Hair got back to his feet and was coming at him again, but he couldn't waste time dodging now.

A second before Long Hair's fist drove into his gut, Shikamaru hit the "execute" button with his thumb.

"Here we go!"

Ino saw the "Network Protected" message disappear from the monitor and leaned forward. She had been waiting on tenterhooks for the firewall to be unlocked.

Orochimaru reacted immediately and began typing at incredible speed.

The time displayed in one corner of the monitor was nine fifty-nine p.m.

"Hurry!" Ino said. "We're out of time!"

"I'm done. These are the signs to undo the ultra particles' seal." Orochimaru zoomed in on the monitor.

Ino wove signs and kneaded her chakra toward her husband halfway across the world.

Sai!

Hey! Can you hear me?!

It was finally here.

Sai heard the familiar voice of his wife in the Land of Redaku. His ears were ringing loudly because of the lack of oxygen, but he could easily pick up his wife's voice echoing directly inside of his head.

I'm going to tell you the signs to release the ultra particles. Horse, Dragon, Pig...

Obeying the voice that flowed through his mind, Sai mustered the last of his chakra.

The blade of the dagger Sasuke had pulled out crackled and flashed, imbued with powerful Chidori electricity. The focal point was turned squarely toward the ultra particles' vessel. It would be an easy feat for Sasuke to break it.

"I told you to stop! Sasuke!" Naruto shouted desperately at the friend who wouldn't meet his eyes.

If the opposite meant sacrificing Sasuke, then a lifetime of never being able to use chakra was a hundred times better

"Sasuke! Listen to me! We're going back down! The mission's over!"

Naruto struggled and kicked with everything he had, and Sasuke drove a serious knee into his solar plexus.

"Just be still, you bumbling fool."

Sasuke pressed Naruto's limp body to his knee and brandished his dagger. *Crack!* Chidori popped, illuminating the air with an intense light, making everything white. The falling tip of the dagger was about to smash the satellite.

Impossibly, in that moment, Naruto's Byakugan saw a change inside of the satellite. The bamboo vessel split open and the metal sphere was full of scattering silver particles.

It opened!

Naruto had no time to communicate that with his mouth. He thrust his own arm out at the tip of the dagger Sasuke was swinging downward. Blood spattered, and the Chidori current passed through Naruto to pierce both himself and Sasuke, knocking off the cement holding the needles in place on their bodies.

Caught off guard, Sasuke hesitated for an instant.

Naruto yanked free the long sword affixed to Sasuke's ankle and kicked the satellite away as hard as he could.

"The seal's undone!" There was no way he was letting Sasuke bring it back with Ame-no-tejikara, so he threw the longsword far away as he shouted with all his might, "You go pick up Sakura and wait down below!"

Without arguing, Sasuke flung out his charred cloak and plummeted downward.

Naruto saw through the gap in the hair that hid Sasuke's face that his expression had softened into something like relief. Then Naruto felt true anger, while also wanting to cry at the same time.

Why is he always thinking only of other people?

Only Sasuke could cause Naruto to feel so angry he could hardly speak and also cry inconsolably when he nearly died. Decades had passed since they first met, and that still hadn't changed even now.

The oxygen supply tube had been yanked out, and he couldn't breathe on his own anymore. Naruto pursed his lips and clung to the satellite.

"Get ready for me, Kurama!" he shouted, letting out all the air in his lungs, until at last he could no longer breathe.

The goggles tore off in the wind and blew away. But he didn't need the Byakugan anymore. He'd already checked that this sphere was full of the silver particles that would wrench open his closed chakra channels.

He threw his head back and headbutted the satellite as hard as he could.

Clang!

The metal body ripped open, and silver particles flew out to envelop Naruto's body. His heart pounded, and his consciousness began to fade.

The pieces of the satellite flew off in new trajectories, with most of them colliding with the Rasenro.

Zznk!

The impact of the satellite remnants passed through the Rasenro to Kakashi and the others at the base. Cracks formed in the earth and wood pillars, quickly spreading out.

"Not good!" Gaara threw up a layer of sand in the air to try and protect the village, but he had used too much of his chakra on the Rasenro. Smashed lumps, chunks of earth, and wood bark rained down.

•

The village of Konohagakure was quiet.

An ordinary weekday evening. Happy laughter spilled out of the izakaya and the Ichiraku stall, while people went about their usual business in brightly lit homes. They had no way of knowing that debris from the Rasenro was closing in on them.

An enormous clod of earth was on the verge of smashing into a house when something white flew in with a *whoosh* and smashed it to pieces. The object spun around as it changed direction like a boomerang and returned to the hand that had thrown it.

Neatly catching the white iron fan was Temari standing on a roof.

"That was a close one. Where'd that even fall from anyway?"

There might be some stuff falling from the sky, so protect the village—Temari wasn't the only one who'd gotten this sketchy instruction from Shikamaru. Tenten, Lee, Kiba, Karui, and Kankuro, who had come running to the Land of Fire with Gaara, were all on standby on the roof.

But there wasn't just one falling object.

Things were dropping down all over from the clouds thinly blanketing the night sky. Chunks of earth and pieces of wood—all of them meters across.

"Wha—"

The shinobi on the rooftop instantly scattered and went after the falling objects. But there were just too many of them. They'd never be able to get them all.

"Not great!" Tenten readied all the tools she had and glared at the sky.

In the next instant, gusts of wind came spinning out from inside the clouds and smashed at least a hundred falling objects simultaneously. The vacuum created by the movement of the wind swept up the shattered fragments, compressed them, and absorbed one fragment after another, not letting a single one fall to the village below.

Odama Rasengan—one of the Seventh Hokage's special Wind Style techniques.

"What? Naruto's here too? No need to worry then." Kiba looked up at the sky, and the tension ran out of his shoulders.

A bright light dropped through a gap in the clouds, looking like a piece of the sun, and landed on top of Hokage Rock. His most powerful battle form, making use of Nine Tails' chakra like it was his own—Naruto in Nine Tails' chakra mode.

Standing on top of the stony face of the Fourth Hokage, Uzumaki Naruto quietly looked out over the village.

Epilogue

The peak of the busy season that year had passed, and for the first time in a long time, Naruto sat down to enjoy his beloved wife's cooking.

"Aaaah. Dinner at home really is the best, huh?"

The dining table was filled with rice, grilled fish, and a number of side dishes, for a simple Japanese meal. The eggplant, lightly stewed with konbu seaweed and a splash of mirin, had been left to chill overnight in the fridge and had thickened up delightfully. The dark purple of the skin transferred to the pale green of the flesh and deepened the flavor. It went perfectly with the smooth white rice.

A flyer for the fireworks festival was sitting on the table. The number of fireworks set off this year would be significantly greater than the five hundred of the previous year, up to an impressive six thousand. The pluripotent applicator Chihare developed had officially been adopted as the triggering explosive for the fireworks, and the result was a dramatic decrease in the cost per firework.

Even now, Chihare was continuing her research at the Kengakuin research institute. Her impressive accomplishments made her the most promising candidate for the next director, but she herself had zero interest in the role.

"I absolutely could not manage human resources or do any of those leadership things. I'm fine being a rank-and-file scientist my whole life, so please give me my own space instead."

Naruto smiled, remembering the tone of her voice. When the Five Kages met and Furieh was arrested, Chihare had been asked if she would be interested in taking over the now vacant director's seat, and she had made that declaration quite flatly. The Five Kages didn't have the authority to assign the labs at the institute, but fortunately, Chihare had been given the private space she wished for and now spent her days immersed in her research, doing whatever she pleased. It seemed that this only exacerbated her disinclination to have anything to do with other people, but the fruits of her research were improving society and having an impact on people.

"Naruto, take your time today, okay?"

"We'll see you later, Daddy!"

Naruto waved goodbye to Hinata and Himawari as they left dressed in summer yukata. Then he checked the time.

"Yikes," he said quietly. He had enjoyed Hinata's cooking a little too much.

I better hurry and get going too. I'm already late.

"Back in the day, there was this weird rumor that the fireworks used people's souls for fuel or something."

"I remember that. Kiba's the one who started that."

Naruto could hear voices talking above him. He carefully climbed the ladder one step at a time but got annoyed halfway up and leaped the rest of the way in a single bound.

"Sorry I'm late!" he said.

"Oh, you're finally here." Sakura pulled a chilled can of cider out of the bag of ice and lobbed it to him. She looked the same as always, having come from work, but Kakashi and Sasuke were in short sleeves, an unusual fashion choice for both of them.

Well, it is hot.

Naruto sat down cross-legged on the roof tiles. He pulled on the tab of the can, and froth came fizzing up and pouring out. He hurried to bring the can to his lips and let the cold liquid trickle down his throat with a satisfying fizz.

"Aah," he sighed happily. "That's the stuff."

"Honestly! You sound like an old man."

Says the woman who's got a skewer of grilled chicken hearts in her right hand and a hunk of dried stingray in her left and four hastily downed and empty cans lined up in front of her, he was about to snark in reply when he heard a whistling sound, so he hurriedly turned his eyes toward the sky.

Boom!

A large circle of red fireworks popped out of the sky and exploded. Thousands of little droplets of flame scattered and spread out before disappearing, tails trailing behind them.

"Where's Hinata?" Kakashi asked as he chewed on a piece of dried stingray.

"She's going to the temple festival with Himawari and her mom friends. She was very excited about catching a lot of goldfish."

"Hinata was? Or Himawari?"

"Both!"

When the goggles broke, the power of the Byakugan returned to Hinata, but unfortunately, ocular jutsu was prohibited at temple festivals in Konoha. Hinata could be surprisingly clumsy, and she always broke the paper goldfish scoop too fast. He wondered how many goldfish she'd come home with that year. He would put some glass beads in the bottom of the fish bowl for her.

Naruto flopped backwards. The roof tiles under his arms were comfortably cool.

The roof of the shed built on the roof of the academy building. He'd passed by this place a few years earlier while playing tag with Boruto and suspected the views would be great from here. It had become the custom for them to have a party here on the night of the fireworks festival. Since no outside personnel were allowed in this place, each of them made maximal use of their ninjutsu to sneak in. If Principal Iruka found them, he would no doubt rap each of them on the head with a heavy fist, but if that happened, then so be it.

After all, this was an incredibly good spot. With no buildings in the way, the whole sky was on beautiful display.

"I ran into Commander Yamato on my way here," he remarked. "Said he was going to guard the gallery seats."

"Sai's on guard duty too. It's a shame he can't come."

Red fireworks spread out above him like an umbrella opening. They kept going up one after another, with barely a space to breathe in between. Blue, white, green, blue. The skyscrapers in the new part of the city reflected the light of the fireworks, each from a slightly different angle, like a kaleidoscope.

"So, listen." Still lying down, Naruto spoke quietly to the backs of the other three. "All of you, thanks. For everything."

No one said anything. The fireworks were loud, so maybe they hadn't heard him.

Naruto glanced at Sasuke, his profile illuminated by the lights in the sky. The area around his right cheekbone was still a little bruised.

That day, after being showered by the ultra particles and returning to the ground, Naruto had forgotten his joy from his chakra returning, grabbed hold of Sasuke, and sobbed.

What were you thinking? You gotta be kidding me. You think I'd be happy with you doing something like that?

Sasuke had quietly allowed himself to be punched, and Kakashi and Yamato—or even Sakura—hadn't tried to stop Naruto, so the shape of a fist was still clear in the bruise on Sasuke's cheek.

Naruto had felt like he would never be able to forgive Sasuke. However.

He guzzled his carbonated beverage and let out a small burp.

The truth was, he couldn't be angry with Sasuke.

I mean, if someone here was in a serious situation, I'd throw down my life for them too. I can't help it. I need them all. Just like they all need me.

Several big fireworks shot up in succession, and then, as if waiting for a brief lull in the smoky sky, a single black kite flew in, a plastic bag hanging from its painted beak. Supplies from Sai.

"Ooh! Beer from the Land of Waves!" Sakura pulled a chilled bottle from the bag and grinned. It was from Ino's current favorite brewer. She quickly poured it into small cups so they could toast, and the tiny heads of foam popped coolly.

"Tell him thanks for us?"

The kite understood Kakashi's words and nodded before spreading its wings and returning to its master.

As if to paint over that figure, another firework shot up into the air. Gold, so bright it made his eyes hurt, popped out all at once and trailed down through the sky like a weeping willow before disappearing.

Boom, boom, boom.

The fireworks kept going up like they were desperately trying to fill the darkness, flashing brightly before fading away.

Naruto threw himself into a sitting position, crushed the empty can, and rolled it behind him.

A warm breeze made Sasuke's long hair dance. Sakura sat hugging her knees to her chest like a child. Master Kakashi was stooped over, the way he always was, standing or sitting.

Naruto would be watching the fireworks with them again next year for sure. And the year after that, and the one after that too. Definitely.

The colors of the fireworks scattered, sank into the night, and vanished.

The foursome clinked the small cups together.

Masashi Kishimoto

Author/artist Masashi Kishimoto
was born in 1974 in rural Okayama Prefecture, Japan.
After spending time in art college, he won the Hop Step Award
for new manga artists with his manga *Karakuri* (Mechanism). Kishimoto
decided to base his next story on traditional Japanese culture. His first
version of *Naruto*, drawn in 1997, was a one-shot story about fox spirits;
his final version, which debuted in *Weekly Shonen Jump* in 1999,
quickly became the most popular ninja manga in Japan.

Born February 13 in
Kanagawa Prefecture. Blood type O.
After graduating from Waseda University,
he began working as a writer.

Jun
Esaka

BORUTO
=NARUTO NEXT GENERATIONS=

CREATOR/SUPERVISOR **Masashi Kishimoto**
ART BY **Mikio Ikemoto** SCRIPT BY **Ukyo Kodachi**

A NEW GENERATION OF NINJA IS HERE!

Naruto was a young shinobi with an incorrigible knack for mischief. He achieved his dream to become the greatest ninja in his village, and now his face sits atop the Hokage monument. But this is not his story... A new generation of ninja is ready to take the stage, led by Naruto's own son, Boruto!

NARUTO

The ninja adventures continue in these stories featuring the characters of **Naruto** and **Boruto**!

A new series of prose novels, straight from the worldwide **Naruto** franchise. Naruto's allies and enemies take center stage in these fast-paced adventures, with each volume focusing on a particular clan mate, ally, team…or villain.